THE VOLUNTEERS

T0100250

PARTHIAN

LIBRARY OF WALES

Raymond Williams was born in the Welsh border village of Pandy in 1921. He was educated at Abergavenny Grammar School and at Trinity College, Cambridge and he served in the Second World War as a Captain in the 21st Anti-Tank Regiment, Royal Artillery. After the war he began an influential career in education with the Extra Mural Department at Oxford University. His life-long concern with the interface between social development and cultural process marked him out as one of the most perceptive and influential intellectual figures of his generation.

He returned to Cambridge as a Lecturer in 1961 and was appointed its first Professor of Drama in 1974. His best-known publications include *Culture and Society* (1958), *The Long Revolution* (1961), *The Country and the City* (1973), *Keywords* (1976) and *Marxism and Literature* (1977).

Raymond Williams was an acclaimed cultural critic and commentator but he considered all of his writing, including fiction, to be connected. *Border Country* (1960) was the first of a trilogy of novels with a predominantly Welsh theme or setting, and his engagement with Wales continued in the political thriller The *Volunteers* (1978), *Loyalties* (1985) and the massive two-volume *People of the Black Mountains* (1988-90). He died in 1988.

THE VOLUNTEERS

RAYMOND WILLIAMS

LIBRARY OF WALES

Parthian, Cardigan SA43 1ED
www.parthianbooks.com
First published in 1978
Reprinted 2024
The Volunteers © Raymond Williams
All Rights Reserved
The Volunteers was first published in 1978
© Raymond Williams Library of Wales edition 2011
Foreword © Kim Howells 2011
All Rights Reserved
ISBN 978-1-914595-92-9
Cover design by www.theundercard.com
Cover image Steve Benbow
Typesetting by www.littlefishpress.com
Printed by 4edge Limited
Published with the financial support of the Books Council of Wales
British Library Cataloguing in Publication Data
A cataloguing record for this book is available from the British Library.

FOREWORD

The coalmining strikes of 1972 and 1974 helped to bludgeon British politics into a crisis as intense as any it had experienced since Suez in 1956. In 1978, when Raymond Williams's *The Volunteers* was published, the success of the National Union of Mineworkers' strike actions caused swathes of trade union leaders to conclude that if the miners could take on and defeat one of the world's biggest industrial employers, then so could other workforces.

The Labour Party found itself besieged by mad, ultra-left factions and activists who assumed that they could ride to power on a wave of industrial unrest, a surge of millennial syndicalism that would sweep away tiresome bourgeois politics. The Tories, initially bewildered at the damage wreaked on the Heath government by the miners' actions, quickly pulled themselves together and started planning how best to defeat militant trade unionism in its strongholds.

By 1978, when *The Volunteers* was published, Jim Callaghan's Labour government enjoyed little respite from the debilitating effects of financial crises, coupled with impossible public and private sector wage demands. The so-called Winter of Discontent heightened the atmosphere of crisis, and it became clear that public opinion was swinging behind the Tories in their determination to curb trade union power. Just months later, in 1979, Margaret Thatcher was elected Prime Minister.

The Volunteers was published a decade after the events of 1968 which had nurtured a generation of unconventional political activists, often from middle-class backgrounds, among student bodies in France, Germany, America and Britain. Ten years on, many of these activists still yearned for fundamental change, though never agreeing on change to *what*, exactly. Each of their factions tended to loathe each other. They expressed their feelings by hurling allegations that their rivals were Stalinist or Trotskyite or Maoist or any one of a score of other deadly isms.

For the Labour Party, the deadliest of these was *entryism*. Incrementally, political activists would capture positions of influence within Labour and trade union branches. Their strategy was to replace social democracy and the 'mixed economy' with revolutionary politics and 'public ownership of the means of production', though they argued endlessly with each other about whether or not 'public ownership' constituted *socialism* or *state capitalism*.

Living and working in Cambridge as one of that university's most distinguished and accessible academics, Raymond Williams was well aware of entryism as one more manifestation of the internecine warfare and sectarianism that the British Left wallowed in. *The Volunteers* sees him exploring the prospect of entryism taken to another level: one that entailed a secret infiltration of revolutionaries to positions of power in the civil service and into the political establishment itself.

He builds the rationale for this tactic slowly and carefully. The novel opens with what appears to have been an attempted assassination of a government minister at St Fagans Folk Museum, near Cardiff, perhaps as revenge for the killing by soldiers of a striking worker at Pontyrhiw, a

South Wales coal depot that resembles Saltley Gate, the scene of a celebrated NUM success in the 1972 miners' strike.

As Williams's cynical, hard-bitten journalist and narrator, Lewis Redfern, investigates the links between the events at Pontyrhiw and St Fagans, he begins to wonder if the attempted assassination was little more than an extravagant ploy by some unseen revolutionary group to remind militant leftists everywhere that 'adventurism', in any form, has led only rarely to political aspirations being realised. It is as if, in the critical years of the late 1970s, Williams is translating into fiction Lenin's warnings of the temptations, weaknesses and dangers of 'infantile leftism', whether it took the form of isolated violence or industrial syndicalism. Williams reminds us that, although the technology of mass communications (and its place in a rapidly changing society) had advanced immeasurably since the Russian Revolution, the Left was still obsessed with fighting the same internecine tactical and theoretical squabbles it had fought with little respite since 1917.

Williams was right, of course. Within six years of Thatcher's election as Prime Minister, the trade union movement had been reduced to a whining shadow of its former bellicose self. The most feared of the unions, the NUM, had been neutered by a combination of Thatcher's vengeful tenacity and skill and Arthur Scargill's megalomania and incompetence.

Williams's perspicacity was obvious to those who knew him in the 1970s. Among the melee of competing slogans, analyses and apocalyptic predictions, his was a quieter, calmer voice, warning us that it was time to wake up to the implications of the enormous changes in the world of communications. In the 1970s he was one of a tiny vanguard of observers who glimpsed with concern, not simply the spectre of a future in which television, radio and newspapers would be dominated by a handful of trans-national companies and media moguls, but also a future in which our culture, and cultures across the world, might be reshaped fundamentally by radical developments in communications technologies.

In the first pages of *The Volunteers* Williams describes how his fictitious 'Insatel Global News Corporation' is prepared to explore the commercial possibilities that might arise from any sector of human activity, from sport to the political underground to financial markets:

'Incidents can occur anywhere,' says Lewis Redfern, describing the news industry, 'but incidents are not news. News depends on a system and the system depends on resources. Insatel gets its resources from advertising, from the big para-national companies, who push the oil and the fibres and the metals... In News Division the political underground runs second only to sport. International terrorist movements, bombs, hijackings, kidnaps: there is no better news in the business.'

Redfern is a 'consultant analyst', a journalist whose role in Insatel is to use his knowledge of subversive political groups to point his colleagues towards the juiciest, most lucrative stories. Normally, Redfern would work to identify the best initial routes before withdrawing to tackle the next story. This time, however, events conspire to begin chipping away at the hard shell he has constructed around himself for his own self-protection. He finds himself unable to make his usual exit as he delves deeper into the possible linkages between the Pontyrhiw killing and the St Fagan's shooting.

Williams doesn't use Redfern to express an opinion, either way, about the tactics of the Volunteers. Nor does he attempt to clarify the ambiguity of Redfern's assessment of the group's strategic aims. It's as if Williams is reminding us that all political actions and gestures are generated and accompanied, always, by ambiguous motives and by unintended consequences, and that only rarely, if ever, is it possible for any of us to be absolutely certain about outcomes. Williams knew, as few others did in the 1970s, that the advances in communication technologies and the media's insatiable and growing hunger for news and controversy might begin to resemble a great cauldron, stewing our diet above a flame of consumer demand. He wouldn't have known, as we do now, that it would result in media corporations having access to the Taliban and Al Qaeda – access denied to the soldiers our state pays to protect us from terrorism. Williams could see the beginnings of these strange and troubling clashes of moral, political and commercial imperatives. He allows Redfern to alert us to these clashes but not to pontificate about them.

Williams describes with skill the world that Redfern moves in. He may have set *The Volunteers* in an imagined 1980s but the novel is a fascinating reminder of the fashions and mores of the 1970s. He contrasts the clothes worn by the novel's dour lefties with the predominating styles of that decade of peacock pop stars, spectacular hair and outrageous tailoring. In one passage he has Lewis Redfern describe the appearance of the sour, humourless Rosa:

> [she] came through the doors and looked around. She was in a grey jacket and jeans: a sort of battledress. I can just remember when the hard types started wearing this, before it spread through the fringe and finally into the fashion photographs.

It is not difficult to recall from that time the beautiful faces of young women and men, tangled up in some Trotskyite sect, who made a fetish of dressing in what they imagined should be the clothes of choice of the working class. The drabber the better. The paler and pastier their skins, the more they believed themselves capable of 'identifying' with the downtrodden masses and of selling on street corners their unreadable propaganda sheets. Some would boast openly that, as creatures of the impending revolution, they were 'dead men walking', like Karl Liebknecht and Rosa Luxembourg, the doomed German revolutionaries.

Perhaps Raymond Williams had Luxembourg in mind when he named the Rosa of the novel. He has Lewis Redfern comparing her with her sister:

> she was really like her sister but in a harder-worn, harder-used copy. The same raven hair, the same big dark eyes, but the skin much flatter and duller, the lower cheeks almost grey, and the features more edgy, the mouth dry.

Williams does not attempt to describe with the same intensity the appearance of industrial South Wales where part of *The Volunteers* is set. Clearly, he knows the landscape but chooses to refer to it only in passing:

> He got up. He looked across at me, then went to the window. 'All quiet in the valley,' he said ironically.
>
> 'It's late.'
>
> 'I don't know. That's Maerdy up here, the street lights. If memories were battalions...'
>
> I didn't answer. I was desperately tired.

'That's another thing... It's interesting. Both your parents went from South Wales to Birmingham. In the thirties, to get work.'

'Yes.'

'So you're at the right distance to get this place wrong,' he said, turning and smiling.

London-based, jet-setter news investigator, Redfern is Welsh by inheritance. Williams describes in the novel Redfern's rebirth as a political radical: not a drab radical, not one in thrall to the 'dead men walking' gangs. When, towards the climax of *The Volunteers*, Redfern comes to give evidence to a key inquiry he wears his denim suit and the batik shirt and refuses the more sober clothes offered to him.

Raymond Williams would have enjoyed placing that luminous little dab of colour. I remember him, in the late 1970s, besieged on a Cambridge stage by revolutionary students and tight-jumpered young lecturers, baying at him for not having mentioned in a talk he had just given the 'fact' that the phenomenally popular American-made programme for children, *Sesame Street*, had allegedly been financed by the CIA.

One young comrade, his pasty face turning red with right-eous Trotskyite indignation, accused Williams of ignoring *Sesame Street*'s role in attempting to heal America and Britain's fractured race relations by including in its line-up fictitious characters of all colours and from all ethnic groups. As the comrade, fist clenched, preached the virtues of encouraging race-based violence for the part it could play in the impending revolutionary struggle, Raymond Williams, smiling slightly, turned his gentle face in my direction and winked.

He was communicating his delight in having the ability to draw such a crowd and to have confirmed, time and again, that his wisdom and insight generated passion and reaction among all who encountered it. Later, over a pint, I had to admit that the counter-revolutionary thrust of *Sesame Street* had passed me by. He smiled and said, 'Me too.'

Kim Howells

PART ONE

1

I was in the air fifty minutes after Buxton was shot. The fax was terse:

MINISTER BUXTON SHOT WOUNDED GROUNDS FAGANS POST CEREMONY SUB RIOT HOSPITALISED CARDIFF ASSAILANT NIL.

In the upstairs office the literati were already translating:

We are just receiving a report that Mr Edmund Buxton, Secretary of State (Wales) in the Financial Commission, has been shot and wounded in the grounds of the Welsh Folk Museum at St Fagans, near Cardiff. Mr Buxton was visiting St Fagans to open a new extension and a newly re-erected building in the Folk Museum, which has extensive open-air exhibits. Earlier today he had presided at a joint session of the Financial Commission and the Financial Board of the Welsh Senate. When he arrived at St Fagans there was a noisy demonstration against him, but this was kept under control by the police. The shooting occurred later, but as yet we have no precise details. There are no reports of the assailant or assailants being detained. Mr Buxton, who is fifty-seven, has been flown to hospital in Cardiff. We shall of course keep you up to date with any further news as it comes in.

As a trailer this would do. Political sensation comes through like that. It might even jerk a few people awake. But almost everything that mattered was still there to find. We can all make the moves to catch history on the wing. But story and

3

history are hard masters, once you take time to stay with them. The literati could fill in. We, downstairs, had to get out and meet the world.

There were eight of us on standby, but there was never any doubt who Friedmann would send. In my three years with Insatel, working out of their London terminal, I have acquired this instant identity: what the ex-intellectuals who run Insatel insist on calling a field. I am what they call their consultant analyst, on the political underground. Insatel is a news and events service. 'Wherever it's happening, with Insatel you're there.' In fact not you, public you; me, public me. Our reporter, your reporter. Wherever it's happening, Mr X marks the spot. But at conferences and in promotions they don't call us all reporters; they call some of us consultant analysts. Reporters are steam people, pre-media people. But we, I, have still to get up and go. If anything happens that sounds political, but that isn't a speech or a party conference, there I am sent: young mole burrowing.

Of course I've accepted the field: the underground field. It is all that keeps me in work. Insatel cost a fortune even before oil and wheat got together to inflate the international economy. As an idea it had belonged to the fast smooth days of universal expansion. Where better to put other people's money than an international television satellite service? After the moonshot, friends, this is the globeshot, the space–time fusion. That is to say, relatively fast television coverage of relatively predictable and relatively accessible events. Most of the events, of course, Insatel arranges itself: all the big sporting contests, the festivals, the exhibitions; Insatel's sponsoring contracts are virtually the only means of finance, in the capitalist world. But somewhere in the margins, on a different principle, other things occasionally

4

happen, and that's where we become relevant, we in News Division. The network already installed for spectacle has this subsidiary facility for unarranged events.

Yet we go up and down, financially, on heavy things like oil and wheat; on cars and trucks and washing machines; on fibres, on metals, on food packaging. To run at all we depend on these other things moving. Incidents can occur anywhere, but incidents are not news. News depends on a system, and the system depends on resources. Insatel gets its resources from advertising, from the big para-national companies, who push round the oil and the fibres and the metals. To run fast we depend on them booming, and lately they haven't been booming. Consultant analysts, by the score, have become, overnight, out-of-work reporters.

Only Insatel's internal ratings saved my own job. In News Division the political underground runs second only to sport. International terrorist movements, bombs, hijackings, kidnaps: there is no better news in the business. Thus even in a (relatively) quiet part of the world, I was a consultant analyst they needed. I can get near these people. I understand their mental processes. I speak their language. Or so Insatel believes.

Nothing is now more respectable, in my kind of world, than an underground past. Until the middle eighties, with new things happening all around them, the media still sent their seasoned old men: tough veterans of the lobbies, the press conferences, and the small-hour ministerial negotiations. They never got within shouting distance. For a start they'd forgotten how to shout. No one now knows what they really did. My private guess is the airport bar, drinking with Immigration and Customs and stolidly alert for a shipment of foreign arms or foreign gold.

5

Then a new generation took over, or, to be strictly accurate, was inserted. There were a good many of us, a few years out of the active movement, needing jobs and a new kind of action. A few of us made it, while most of the generation drifted, fairly happily, into teaching and publishing and the respectable agencies. We lost touch with them, easily. But we didn't lose touch with the few who were sticking it out: squatting, translating, organising, splitting, regrouping, marching, researching, recruiting, being recruited. That is still our world, we still think in its ways, though the consequent distinction between observer and participant has become, to put it mildly, a bit of an issue.

The really hard groups never touch us; we have to dig for them. Even when they issue their distant, quasi-official communiqués, they don't give them to us, who would know what questions to ask. They give them straight to the establishment, who wrinkle their long noses but still take them at face value, like all the other official handouts they're used to reporting. But many groups that appear quite hard do accept us, circumspectly, for what they can get, and that, of course, is publicity, visibility, some minimal sign that all that sustained, dedicated, voluntary work is having a little registered effect: of course distorted by the media but present in the media; a bitter habituation; the best exposure you can get.

All the soft and mixed groups come out to greet us, of course. When we arrive, they've arrived. 'Sure,' they say, 'Insatel defines the spectrum, but look right into it, look at the contradictions of the system. It picks us up and distorts us; it also picks us up and connects us. The hard Right understands this; it wants all this coverage banned. And that's correct, because the whole situation is so dynamic and contradictory that our paradoxical news value is a danger to

6

it. Once we're seen as existing, we become a real possibility, outside the orthodox channels. Dialectically, in fact, the media use us and we use the media.' Nice sensible people otherwise. Much too nice to contradict.

It wasn't a soft group that had shot Buxton. Friedmann half expected me to solve it right there in his office, but he was very jumpy because he knew he'd just lost. Two days earlier, I had put this up to him. I hadn't known what was coming, but I'd seen something coming. I'd said that to let Buxton go to Wales, within four months of the events at Pontyrhiw (where a worker had been killed and eight others wounded, as the army moved in to occupy a power depot; moved in, it was widely suspected, on direct orders from Buxton), was provocative in anybody's language: anybody, that is, except the people who arrange these affairs, who are so much inside their tight little world they think public life is a sort of timetable: official visits must be paid; normal civil service must continue. I'd shown Friedmann leaflets of the huge demonstration that had been called for St Fagans when Buxton was due to arrive. I'd said it might be anything, though the most I'd then imagined was some kind of riot. He'd pushed it back at me. 'You tell me, Lewis, the difference between these heaving images you'd get and any Welsh rugby crowd, singing for dear heart before some match or other.'

He was having to digest that dismissive rhythm now. It had been his judgement, as Senior Analyst, that a factory occupation in West Bromwich was much more significant.

'Tell me the difference,' I'd echoed, 'between that and any library footage of locked gates and pickets.'

'No,' he'd said, 'this may be different, Lewis. I just have that feel it may be different.'

7

His feel had been rough. West Bromwich was respectable, by now in effect constitutional. Everything visible and reportable even finished early. And St Fagans, meanwhile, had erupted: the first political shooting in Britain this century. Either I could solve it then and there, or I could turn round and take his jet. The offer indicated the depths of his disgust and remorse. That plane is his ego – even to ask for it, normally, amounts to personal assault. But here he was telling me to take it. He had been wrong so badly that I could have chartered a flying carpet and six gilded flamingos, so long as I got there.

'The crew's already moving,' he said, with what would have been reproach if he'd quite had the nerve.

I took a car to the field, and was driven right up to the waiting plane. I enjoyed this routine immensely. Now there was only the actual work.

2

I went straight from the airport by air taxi to St Fagans. A police headquarters had been set up in the castle: that kind of instinctive move which is always reassuring; it lets you know where you are, and what kind of world is assumed. Down to quite small details, in fact. The police themselves were in the office and the hall; the press room was in that old kitchen, with its museum collection of ancient spits and utensils; stone-cold, hollow, but with plenty of room for menials like us. We sat at the plain, scrubbed tables, facing the collections of old ladles and carving knives, in a kitchen which had everything but food.

We got a first briefing, towards midnight, from Superintendent Walter Evans. It was superficially very clear, in fact very vague. There was a large map of the immediate area: the castle, the main museum building, the park with its open-air reconstructions. Alongside it was a timetable of the main events. The Superintendent took us through both, and from this, and from what I had got earlier from the local reporters, an outline of the story emerged.

After the day's meetings in Cardiff, Buxton was due to open, at seven o'clock, the new wing of the main museum building. He would then go on into the park to open the latest re-erected building: the eighteenth-century Customs House and Harbour Master's Office from Aberesk, which had been taken down and removed during the construction

9

of the new marina. The new wing was easily guarded, and Buxton landed by helicopter, straight from the joint session, in a cleared area of the car park. Six hundred police formed a square around the landing area. In the wing itself there were only carefully selected and invited guests.

Most of the programme had been known in advance, and one of the largest demonstrations ever seen in South Wales had gathered around the car park, after a march from Llandaff. Even before Pontyrhiw, Buxton had been unpopular, but then it had been a more ordinary politics. Since the Welsh Senate was established, in the initial devolution of powers under the second coalition government, the Financial Commission has been the political storm centre. For what the devolution said, in effect, was this: you can govern yourselves, on this range of issues, within the limits of the money we are prepared to allocate to you. The important effect of the Senate was to make this process, which in different ways had been there all the time, very much more visible and contested. It became apparent, above all, in the figure of the Financial Commission's Secretary of State (Wales). He was supposed to be an impartial figure, indeed not a figure but figures: a rational accounting procedure. But of course he was political, and through his office flowed all the fierce currents of political conflict between an impatient people and a constrained, fatigued and impoverished administration. Anyone holding Buxton's position was then a marked man in Wales: marked and resented if not actively hated.

The passage from resentment, however fierce, to what can properly be called hatred, depended, of course, on a single event. The army's attack at Pontyrhiw, which ended with the death of Gareth Powell, would have led, in any case, to a very deep bitterness. But when the public inquiry opened, and the army's evidence was given, it became more and more likely that what had been widely suspected was true: that Buxton was involved, not just as an adviser, or as the responsible minister visiting a trouble-spot, but in effect as a commander, as chief strategist. This was of course denied; there was no real evidence of it, of a kind you could prove. But still he was seen, throughout Wales, at the time of his visit, as the man primarily responsible for that bloody Thursday and indeed as the murderer of Gareth Powell.

It was then extraordinary, as I had told Friedmann, that within four months he was again appearing in public in Wales. Of course his work required him to go regularly to Cardiff, to the offices of the Senate and the Assembly. But that can be and usually is hermetic. Demonstrations, repeatedly, had tried to intercept him, but there was the smooth police passage from train to car, or, more often, the arrival by helicopter in the closed grounds. His visit on 9 July was primarily for a meeting of this kind: a joint session of the Financial Commission and the Financial Committee of the Senate. His visit to the Folk Museum had been arranged for many months, from before the confrontation at Pontyrhiw. I have no idea whether he was urged to cancel it. He was bound to have been aware of the feeling against him. As we all now know, he went on with it. He said in a statement, when he arrived in Cardiff, that he was in the habit of fulfilling his normal engagements. Whether this was courage or contempt for the feeling against him there is no easy way of knowing. I would still call it courage; a kind of courage: a kind characteristic of one sort of ruling-class man, in whom physical bravery can never quite be separated from the associated emotions of arrogance and contempt. Yet

11

Buxton is not, by origins, a ruling-class man. He is an educational meritocrat, a career politician, who moved from the public bureaucracy, where he was a scientific officer, to Parliament and the administration: an effective and successful move in his mid-thirties. So it is not his inherited class, or any kind of inherited property or position, that has produced his undoubted authoritarian character. He is that now more dangerous kind of man, whose authority and whose ruthlessness derive from his absolute belief in his models: rational models of what is and must be. It is never Buxton you challenge; it is fact and reason itself. Of course the version of fact and reason that the administration has selected: the Buxton version.

The march from Llandaff had been noisy but straightforward. It was in the wait at St Fagans, in the crowding along the roads and approaches, in the sudden barrier of the police guarding the landing area, that tempers began to rise. When the helicopter was sighted there was one of those heaves and surges which can happen in crowds; people pushed or were pushed against the triple lines of police; there were scuffles and arrests; a police horse was brought down. As the helicopter landed, with its shattering noise, it even looked for a time as if the crowd would break through. The noise of the shouting, when the helicopter's engines suddenly died, was like an explosion: a sustained explosion. Buxton got out, briskly, and waved to the crowd. He was smiling. It is said that we smile when we are either pleased or nervous; this was perhaps something else, but it came through as extraordinary bravado, and the shouting changed its pitch, became higher and harsher. But then it was over. He turned and went into the new wing. The police lines held. There was a sudden silence.

12

It was the next few minutes that may have turned things. The crowd, or most of them, would have stayed anyway. They could demonstrate again when Buxton came out and took off. But the police seem to have chosen that moment of relative lull and uncertainty to try to push them back, to regain the few yards they had lost. It was an extraordinary decision, for it fired the crowd at once. I say the crowd, and it was, indeed, a collective phenomenon. But when you are in such a crowd, and the pressure starts, from any direction, you are not acting according to some crowd mentality, you have to try to hold your ground, keep your feet, stay close to your friends. The physical pressures and cross-pressures build up very quickly. What may look from outside to be some kind of mass phenomenon is from inside a series of sharp small movements, almost all of them defensive, and the step to avoid becomes, without intention, the step towards another which in turn sets him moving, and the surge can begin. There was the worst fighting then. The people in front had literally nowhere to go: the police were trying to push them back, but behind them were thousands of crowded people, almost all simply trying to hold their own ground. It was inevitably rough; many people were hurt, and the police, to say the least, were at full stretch – indeed only just holding their lines.

It isn't clear, and Superintendent Evans wouldn't make it clear, whether the guard on Buxton, when he went on to open the re-erected Customs House, was intended, from the beginning, to be so small. My own guess is that, without the fighting, it would have been somewhat larger, but not significantly. For that trip into the park had not really been publicised, although it could easily have been found out. Under the pretext of the ceremony of the opening of the wing, the

13

grounds of the park – indeed everything except the castle – had been cleared and closed to the public from five o'clock. And it was then a question of how the danger was perceived. The demonstration was obviously dangerous; so everything else was not, or was minor by comparison. It is of course easy to be wise after the event. In fact, as the surge and the fighting continued, few extra men could be spared. And with the park fully cleared and closed to the public, it must have seemed an oasis of quiet, a rural and pastoral tract, when Buxton left the new wing, where some of the guests, especially the women, stood looking down with fascination at the surges of the crowd, and went through, by a side door, to the winding paths of the open museum. There were at first eleven people with him, in the leading group, only three of them policemen; this group, later, began to spread out. Up to fifty other people were following, trailed out, along the sunlit paths. They went down past Kennixton Farmhouse, with its whitewashed walls, its thatched roof, its small windows. They passed the boundary stone and the tollhouse; on their right were the dark boulder walls of Llanfadyn Cottage. It could have been a stroll through a village on a summer evening: the houses so quiet, the fine high trees, the birds singing. Ahead of them, along the path, was Cilewent Farm: the old moorland longhouse from Dyffryn Claerwen in Radnor, the fine sandstone of the gable wall very light in the sun. Beyond it, to the right, was their destination, the old Customs House and Harbour Master's Office: a world of recollection, of order, of conventional memories and signs. The angry crowd was far behind them, held and pushed by the police. It would have been taken as an interval, a relaxing, unguarded, delightful moment.

Within the next two minutes Buxton was shot. Now that it

14

has happened it seems very obvious, with that dreadful obviousness of the absorbed fact. But at the time it was wholly astonishing: an absolute surprise. Not only in itself, as a physical fact, in that quiet parkland, that simulated peace of a village – but even more as a social fact, a political fact, for this was the first shooting of a political leader, on the British mainland, in this century. It is known that it happens elsewhere; it was not believed that it would happen here.

His assailant was waiting behind the Cilewent Farmhouse. It is worth considering his position. By this early account he was alone behind the farmhouse, within a quarter of a mile of a noisy political demonstration and on a day when the police had gathered to protect his intended victim. He could have had no means of knowing, until the last few minutes, how many people, and how many police, would accompany Buxton to the opening of the Customs House. He could not even have known which way they would come, except very generally. He must have been prepared, until the last few minutes, to shift his own position. And this was not, after all, a familiar type of attack. We know about ambush, from the cover of a hedge or a building, or in darkness. We know about the shot from a distance: the high window, the balcony, the bridge, the passing car. In one way or another, if he had been following Buxton about, any of these other methods could have been chosen. Most obviously, of course, the man stepping from a crowd, or firing from a crowd: that, perhaps, is the most available method of all; it has happened so often, though it carries greater risk than the others.

But risk, evidently, was not the first thing in his mind. The risk he actually chose to take was extraordinary, for he was in effect alone, in an open space, under some degree of alert, and his chances of getting away with it must on any calculations have been small. Now that we know that it happened we have to make our calculations again, but whichever way you look at it the risk seems fantastic. People were already saying, that night, that the risk was so great that he was willing or even intended to be captured; even that being captured would have been the true completion of what he was doing. From that reading, of course, all kinds of psychological and similar deductions would follow. But we have to stick to what actually happened. In those few decisive minutes, which as we can all now see had been carefully planned, he clearly knew what he was doing and what he would do next, and the fact remains that, by whatever degree of luck or accident, he both shot Buxton and got clear away.

He must have been in his final position when they were coming up the path from the boundary stone and the tollhouse and Llanfadyn Cottage. The long path is straight, under the trees. Just short of Cilewent it divides; it goes back to the left, through the wood, to the Cockpit and the Tannery; to the right it turns towards Cilewent and the new site of the Customs House and so along to Abernodwydd Farmhouse and Capel Pen-rhiw. So he would have known that the party must bear to the right. There is then a minor entrance, only a few yards off the path, to Cilewent Farmhouse itself. You can turn in and enter the long house, through the stable door or beyond it the main door. At the end of the gable wall which is facing you, as you approach the house, is a low, wooden rail fence and gate, and beyond these a garden. It was as the party reached the minor entrance, moving on towards the Customs House, that a smoke-bomb exploded behind them, on the grass at the edge of the path.

This came as a total surprise. Nobody saw it thrown, and some who were there were quite certain that it must have been thrown by a second man, perhaps from the cover of the trees where the main path divides. But Superintendent Evans believed this unlikely. It was in this area that the police, who were following Buxton, were immediately able to carry out a search, and they found nobody. The smoke bomb must have been held in the hand until the last moment, for it was emitting heavy orange smoke from the instant when it was seen. Indeed the first conclusion was that it had been exploded *in situ*, rather than thrown, so quick was the emission. But the police believed that with the type of bomb used this was not technically possible. It must then have been thrown, and it is practically certain that it was thrown by the young man who had been waiting behind the Cilewent Farmhouse.

The direction of the wind, which was a point or two north of west, had been carefully allowed for in choosing the point of impact, and the throw was then extraordinarily accurate. It has been said that this too was luck, but that sounds like an excuse (and there were, for obvious reasons, very many excuses). The dense and acrid smoke had the effect of temporarily isolating the leading group: Buxton himself, his private secretary Eyre, the Senate official Parry and the museum guide Jones. In detail, of course, this could not have been calculated, and it may indeed have been luck that in those first moments the police were temporarily cut off. But the surprise was so complete that there was not even panic, only a shocked immobility. Then a further smoke-bomb exploded, along the line of the rail fence. For a decisive minute, that whole area, from the fence along the gable wall and to the junction of path and entrance where Buxton and

17

the three others were standing, was screened by the heavy smoke.

It was at that moment that the young man appeared. He was very clearly remembered by the four people who saw him. He was of medium height, wearing a bright orange mountain cape; it was this flash of colour that first fixed in their minds. He was wearing dark glasses and a peaked blue denim cap. His fair hair was long and he had a beard and moustache. He was through the gate when they really saw him. He was carrying a shotgun. He moved to get a clear sight on Buxton, who had been momentarily screened by Parry. Then he shot from about seven yards, with both barrels. Buxton cried out and fell.

Everyone now was shouting. Other people were running forward, through and around the smoke. It was the guide Jones who ran towards the young man first; both Eyre and Parry had turned to help Buxton. Immediately after the shots the young man was running, taking his first steps backwards until he was at the gate. He slammed the gate shut and threw the shotgun at Jones. It hit him on the shoulder and arm. While he was briefly stopped, he saw the young man turn and run west, into the covering smoke of the second bomb. Jones is very certain about this. But by the time he had recovered, and got the gate open, there was no further sign of the attacker. Jones ran in the direction in which he had seen him start.

There were soon other pursuers: Eyre and two of the police, Inspector Harries and Sergeant Dean. They made for the back of the farmhouse and the sheep pens behind it. There was nobody in sight. But beyond the sheep pens, where a small path enters the boundary strip of trees, they found an orange cape, which Eyre at once recognised. The whole search was then concentrated in that direction, along the path and through the trees and on to the track which runs outside the line of the park. They went along the track, in both directions, and others were sent into the same area, as soon as they arrived. By radio message, from Inspector Harries, all ways out of this area were quickly blocked by police cars.

Jones, meanwhile, had gone in a different direction. He was no more successful than the others in seeing the young man again. He is a man of over sixty; it is clear that he kept up the presumed chase as long as he could, but this was not very far; and with no sight of his quarry, and with the wide stretches of woodland beginning almost at once to the west, he could not know which way to go on. He at last turned back. The search to the north was now well under way. The finding of the cape did not persuade Jones that he was wrong about the direction of flight, but he was shocked and exhausted and after making his statement he was driven home.

In the remaining two hours of daylight the search continued. Nothing more was found: Superintendent Evans was very frank about this. He had the confidence, after all, of the tangible evidence – the cape and the shotgun; the detailed physical description. He gave the impression that the case was well in hand and that an arrest was only a matter of time. I listened, politely, with the rest, but when he had given the latest information on Buxton I knew that was all we would get.

Buxton had been shot in both legs, mainly below the knees. There was no danger to his life, but he was crippled and in great pain. Someone ran back to the new wing and got the pilot of the helicopter. It made the short journey to where Buxton was lying, on the grass in front of the farmhouse, with Parry's jacket under his head and a woman's coat over his legs. He was lifted on board, and the helicopter took him to hospital in Cardiff. A medical bulletin said that he was receiving emergency treatment.

I remembered the fax: Minister Buxton Shot Wounded Grounds Fagans Post Ceremony Sub Riot Hospitalised Cardiff Assailant Nil. Apart from some picturesque detail, Friedmann's precious jet hadn't led me to much more. With the exception, of course, of the figure who dominated the briefing, the figure so clearly lodged in everyone's mind: the young man in the orange cape, with dark glasses and a blue denim cap, and with long fair hair and beard and moustache. When I found myself smiling, as I replayed this description, I got up and went out. If I had stayed the smile would have been misunderstood.

3

I showed my pass to get out of the castle. It was ironic, that way round, but the police were taking no chances. Everybody moving, anywhere in the area, was being stopped and questioned. Barriers had been set up on all the roads out of St Fagans, as well as in the immediate area of the search. On the wrong side of the roadblocks there had been anything from fifteen to twenty thousand people. By the time I got there most of them had got through, but it had been a painfully slow business and there were still plenty of people around. I got down to the area of one of the roadblocks, again after several challenges, with torches being shone in my face. There was a group of about thirty people on the museum side, where they had been told to wait.

They had all been on the demonstration. All of them wore the Pontyrhiw Campaign badges: either the popular model – red, on white: *Pontyrhiw* – or, quite frequently, the militant version – black on white: *Arrest Buxton*. I talked to a boy and a girl – they were both under twenty – who were wearing the militant badges: in fact the girl was wearing three of them, in line down her cardigan. I got their story of what had happened back in the car park. They had known nothing about the shooting for more than an hour. The first sign of something unexpected was when the helicopter took off, before Buxton's return. They saw it rise and fly off towards the north-west. They knew now that it was going to pick up Buxton, who was lying wounded: it was not generally known, even now, how seriously. It was only after he had been flown back to hospital, and after the police had taken time to put up roadblocks behind them, that an announcement was made that Buxton had been shot.

It was an extraordinary moment. As the message came booming and crackling over the police loudspeakers, which that whole evening they had stood opposing, there was first an angry shout, as Buxton's name was mentioned, and then, after only the briefest interval, when it was said that he had been shot, there was an extraordinary cheer. They were very frank about this: absolutely honest with themselves and with each other, though it was obvious they weren't now proud of it. However brief the cheer had been, however momentary and regretted and checked a reaction, it was a sign that a gap had closed, or was about to close, in many thousands of minds: a critical gap between words and actions. For indeed it had been an exultant cheer: they made that quite evident. It was one of those occasions when deep feeling comes through, without second thought. Thousands of them, standing there, were, at first anyway, glad that Buxton had been shot. They were not stunned into silence or shocked by this sudden climax. They were instantly glad, and they cheered.

But then, quite quickly, their mood had changed. It would be easy to say that they realised what they were doing, even that a gap showed itself again, as they made the translation from Buxton deserving to be shot to a man lying on the ground with his flesh torn and bleeding. Certainly, later, they reflected on the physical fact; they saw and in some degree felt the wounds. This was still obvious as the girl, Megan,

22

was speaking about it, several hours later. But the real reason for the cheer ending was a different emergency. The police had taken up positions behind them. They were blocked in. The loudspeakers announced that everyone would be stopped and searched before being allowed to leave the area. The cheer ended, the boy – Trevor – said, because they had other things to do. It was all so chaotic, with everyone trying to talk or shout at once, and with small groups forming to make their own plans, that nobody could say what the crowd decided; they reacted in different ways. But the march organisers had the loudspeakers. After only a brief delay, they reminded everyone that this was a non-violent demonstration. They urged everyone to leave, when instructed, in an orderly way, and to cooperate in any reasonable measures required by the police. This in its turn provoked some anger. One group struggled for a microphone and even seized it for some moments, urging everyone to stand their ground, to let the police come to them, and to give no information beyond what was legally necessary. Trevor heard another group making plans to break out, to smash the police roadblocks and to 'finish what had been started'. But there were too many people for any particular faction to get effective control, and perhaps the decisive fact was the sheer physical congestion. There was only one road out of the car park, and there were many thousands of them. They were like a football crowd, including knots of difference or of angry dissent, but constrained by their physical position: only the one road out and the police blocking it. It was an immensely prolonged and dreary business: it was gone nine o'clock before even the car park was cleared. And there was already some fighting. Several groups charged the barrier; some seemed to have got through. But meanwhile, methodically, hundreds of young men were being picked out of the slowly moving crowd and taken down the lane that ran back to the castle. At the time they had not understood how they were being selected. Nobody in the crowd yet knew about the description of the assailant: the young man behind the Cilewent Farmhouse; the young man in an orange cape and a blue cap, the young man with dark glasses, long fair hair and a beard and a moustache. But of course the police knew: the easy description had been circulated. Within half an hour it became known by most of the people waiting their turn to get out. And then look at it, Trevor said, from the police point of view: the cape and cap could be chucked, the dark glasses put away. What they really had was a fair bearded young man, and you can imagine how many there were of those.

'It was bloody chaos, mun. Detaining and trying to identify half the population.'

'A quarter more like,' Megan said, still intent on absolute accuracy.

'Too bloody many, anyhow,' Trevor said. He was himself very dark, but long-haired and bearded. Megan, who was tiny, had long fair hair.

Anyway, slowly it had cleared. But after the first hour or so the word came back that there was a change of policy on the barrier. They were mostly just taking names and addresses of anyone they thought looked suspicious, and not only fair-haired young men. You could see their difficulty. They were being overwhelmed by sheer numbers. But the word also came back that there were different people on the checkpoint, just behind the police: plain-clothes men, Special Branch. The identifications were various, but the change was quite clear. People were being picked out, and asked to wait, on a different principle: anybody whose face was known, as Trevor put it naively. We seemed now to be in the last stages of this.

I had got enough of the picture. I said goodnight to Trevor and Megan and got out my pass again. It was brusquely enough received by one of the men on the barrier, who told me to get through and keep going: they had no room for reporters here. This suited me. I wanted to get in to the city and check the real action. I got a lift not far down the road. Everybody, that night, was very generous with lifts.

Nobody was generous with much else. At the central police station, where most of those detained had been taken, it was all firmly behind the desk. But it was clear enough what was happening: routine had taken over. The people who had been picked out were being asked about their movements, and they were all no doubt replying that they had been on the demonstration and had not at any time left it. This would need corroboration: who had they been with? Had anyone else seen them? Imagine that with the remnant of a fair-sized football crowd! In most cases they had simply been with each other or with people they'd never seen before who had now gone home. All this was being written down, in deceptive detail, because it sustained the illusion of relevant inquiry. If they had been less busy the police would surely have realised that the chance of that young man having deliberately gone back into the crowd at the demonstration was so very small that it could be set aside, and a lot of time saved. But the procedure is never as closely related to purpose or judgement as that. It is really a standardised form of response to trouble, this cold, polite, generalised questioning, defining the troublesome public from which, somehow, the disturbance has come.

25

You could actually smell this feeling in the otherwise sterilised atmosphere of the station. But beyond it what was really being assembled was a list of names, and this would be going back to the real investigators, who would be checking them against their own lists.

There are three of these: their existence, of course, is always officially denied. There is Regional List F, of politically suspect individuals; List B, of subversive organisations and their principal members; and, most sensitive, List 21 (the number is from a now obsolete Home Office regulation), of individuals 'qualified' (as it is quaintly put) for surveillance – there are categories within this, and in most cases actual surveillance only happens when there is some specific alert. The lists vary in quality, but if any of the really hard groups or individuals are on any of them it is mostly by chance, from some old or innocent membership of some quite different organisation. Until the middle seventies this wasn't so much the case, because the political situation was different and there was a fair continuity from the radical groups of the sixties, (though with some ludicrous insertions; campaigning ecology groups, for example, got on to the lists alongside the Marxist factions and the peace campaigns, bringing with them a larger than usual quota of Justices of the Peace, impeccably married ladies and ministers of religion). But the lists had been assembled in that now obsolete situation, when the political map was fairly clear. Since the fundamental changes of the late seventies and early eighties the territory is very much harder to map, and the authorities are badly out of touch, at the same time, ironically, as they are more vigilant and intrusive.

For what it is worth, that map is my livelihood. In this case some of its features were clear: all the Welsh nationalist and radical organisations were obvious elements of it, and especially of course the Pontyrhiw Campaign. The road to the Cilewent Farmhouse led from the Pontyrhiw depot, anybody would have to conclude. With several thousand badges screaming at them all evening, the police needed no help to reach that conclusion. But that would be the difficulty, for the Pontyrhiw Campaign was no marginal sect: it was the response of a whole community, a whole country, to the shooting of one of its young men. That, more than anything else, is the way the map has changed, requiring a quite different projection.

Anyway, at three in the morning it was obvious, and welcome, that nothing was going to get out past that guarded desk. I found a hotel and turned in, with an alarm call for seven. All the real investigation remained to be done.

4

The next morning was clear and sunny. I got a car back out to St Fagans and marvelled again at how good this society is at restoring a surface order. Nobody would have known, in that early July sunlight, with the roads cleared to their everyday appearance, the barriers taken down and transported away, the police so unobtrusive in their patrol cars at the junctions, that just overnight this had been the place of a seething crowd, of arrests and searches, of an angry demonstration and a political shooting. The museum car park had been swept and was now being watered. The white lines of the parking spaces were its primary inhabitants, all the movement and shouting of the great crowd gone. The few official press cars might have been there on ordinary business. Only an improvised notice at the turnstiles – Museum Temporarily Closed – showed anything out of the way, and its message was characteristic: something had happened to disturb a tranquil order, but it was only temporary; every routine could be confidently expected to resume, in due course, at the appointed time.

I looked in at the press room at the castle. There was hardly anyone there; nothing was yet happening. I went through to the great terrace and looked down into the park. It was restful and beautiful: the trees just turning from their brightest green, the water lively in the sunlight, with the birds flying over it. The full improbability of the whole scene struck me very forcibly. What a place, after all, for an event like this! A political shooting, from the raw hard world of modern industrial struggle, had taken place here, in a folk museum. The very incongruity, after the first surprise (which looking down from that terrace at the peaceful trees and the water kept returning, mysteriously, as if only these things were real and all the rest was nightmare), had, in the end, a certain point. It was just the improbable conjunction, the bringing together of apparently separate parts of our life, that made it significant. What this place offered, after all, was a version of the life of a people: a version, characteristically, that attracted official visits. And then what had poured into it, roughly and incongruously, with this lingering shock of surprise, was another version, another practice, of the life of the same people. The clash of scene and action was then the first thing to grasp. To understand that would be to begin to come nearer. But even while I came to this conclusion, standing quietly on the terrace, another part of my mind was saying all the time: 'This is a lovely summer morning; here are trees and water and birds; none of the rest matters, let it go to hell its own way.'

The feeling was so strong that it started me walking, in effect without decision. I had picked up a guidebook and map in the castle. I began going round, as if nothing had happened. At every turn of the paths the sense of pleasure and of strangeness was again confirmed. It was so good, so quiet. Across at the Cilewent Farmhouse, where this strange event had occurred, a surface order had been restored: the area roped off; the plain-clothes policemen inside it, measuring. Measuring as the response to every disturbance, every accident: is it not always how such events are seen? They were measuring the scene of an exceptional event, but you could have believed, watching them across the fine grass, that they were measuring for a new path, or for a barn going up: the innocent ceremonies of building a country.

I kept away from Cilewent. I walked round the rest of the grounds. I took in the feel of the place, its pleasure and its strangeness. It was only when I had walked for more than an hour that the strong feeling faded, and a line of thought came back: a line, a point of view, after the hour's randomness, the unsorted, unsortable impressions, the flow of a body in a place. Yet it always comes back. The ordered world is always re-enacted. I stood back and tried to see it.

The Welsh Folk Museum is a translation, culturally and physically, of a Scandinavian form. It offers to show the history of a people in its material objects; tools, furniture, arms, fabrics, utensils. In the main museum building these are shown in the conventional way, by a labelled display of each category. But in the open museum there are houses, barns, a chapel, a tollhouse, a cockpit, rural factories: all acquired in different parts of Wales, taken down and re-erected in the grounds of the open museum. The objects which in the museum building are displayed as abstract categories are in the open museum restored to their contexts: axes, spades, chairs, beds, tables, pans, spits, pews, looms, vats are in their places of use, as if the men and women who made them and used them and lived by them had just left them or laid them down. It is an active material history of the people of Wales: up to a certain point.

But, first, this is an active history only of *rural* Wales: of farms and cottages, and of the early industries of tanning and weaving. All the later history, of the majority of Welsh people, is simply not seen: the mining townships, the quarrymen's villages, the iron and steel works settlements;

the pitcage, the picks and shovels, the slate-saws, the chisels, the masks of the blast furnacemen, the wrenches, the hoses, the grease-guns. The idea that the museum embodies is of an old Wales, still in part surviving, but with all the modern realities left outside in the car park, or brought inside only in the toilets which have replaced the privies. That is why it is called a *folk* museum. Folk is the past: an alternative to People.

Then again: the material history. It is pleasant, of course, to walk through the farmhouses and the stables and the dairies and the kitchens: to see the beds, chairs, cradles, knives, churns, presses, flails, coppers, stoves, casks, lying all so naturally and so clean to hand. But there are no people here, except as spectators and guides. There are no marks of use – the crumpled sheets, the stained knives. There are a few sheep in the pens, a few flowers and herbs in the gardens, but no muck in the drains, no ashes on the hearths. For this is a cleaned-up history, of only part of the material. The people are implied, by the shapes of their tools and their furniture, but are essentially absent, not only physically but in the version that is given of them: polished shells of their lives.

Then finally: the real history of this folk museum. It is laid out in the grounds of a castle. The castle and grounds were the 'most generous gift' of the Earl of Plymouth. If you go straight to the grounds you get one idea of a people: the stone and whitewashed farmhouses, the boulder cottages, the bare little chapels that doubled as schools. It is a real history; it can still be seen, in very similar shapes, in parts of Powys and Gwynedd and Dyfed, and indeed in some areas of Gwent. In those farms and cottages and chapels a real history was made and lived, and is still made and lived.

But lived, throughout, under a definite shadow, and to see this you must come in by the other entrance. It is by descent a Norman castle: 'bestowed upon Sir Peter le Sor by Robert Fitzhamon, the Norman conqueror of Glamorgan'; passing by marriage to the le Veles, and so on through a tangle of marriages and purchases – purchased marriages and betrothed purchases – to the third Earl of Plymouth and the ninth Baron Windsor. It is a gross building: a fortress that has been turned, through the centuries, into a country house. It is then as real a part of the history as the isolated farms and the cottages, and it is right that it should stand there, if only to show that this is more than the story of a folk; it is the story of a people.

You can queue up now for tea – English teas 70p, Welsh teas 95p – in a part of the castle. You can stand on the terrace, above the fishpond, and look down on that park with its preserved and isolated remnants. But you can also hear voices from behind you: the voices that you do not hear in the scrubbed and polished empty rooms of the farms and cottages: voices speaking of tribute and of taxes and of rents; voices speaking in different languages, Norman-French and English but in the farms and cottages the native language, the language of the comrades, the Cymry; the native language, become foreign and called, in that Saxon word for foreigner, Welsh. In that school down there, teachers paid by the English hung rectangular pieces of wood, the Welsh Nots – there are several preserved in the museum – around the necks of children who came from their homes and spoke with the tongues of their fathers and mothers.

There are other voices that might be heard on that terrace. In the Civil War, the greatest battle in Wales was fought in this place, and it was won by the Parliament; the Royalists were routed and three thousand taken prisoner. In the nineteenth century this castle was absentee property: a school and a Sunday school found shelter inside it; people moved in from the village while their cottages were being repaired. A different life was asserting itself; the balance of forces was being altered. For by now, up the valleys, a modern Wales was being built. From the farms and the cottages came the ironworkers, the miners, the steelmen, fighting endless battles against the new barons, the coal and iron masters; and though the farms and cottages were still being worked and lived in, there was this new history and this new struggle, and the people changed. In the museum building you can go from the games – the bando and quoits – past the finely carved lovespoons and the skull ribbons of Mari Llwyd, past the little magical crosses of elder and the corn mare's tails and the polished oak and brass dressers, to the Schedule of Sentences at the Glamorgan Assizes, the deaths and the gaolings and the beatings, and among them – Numbers 12 and 14 – the sentences passed after the Merthyr riots of 1831. On Lewsyn yr Heliwr (Lewis Lewis) and Dic Penderyn (Richard Lewis): guilty of high treason. Lewsyn yr Heliwr transported; Dic Penderyn hanged.

In the tidied farms, among the casks and the presses, you could forget this history, on an ordinary day. But today was not ordinary. Today made these other connections: the connections to Pontyrhiw. What had started there had come back to this folk museum, not as an exhibit but as an action, bursting in on its peaceful and arranged order: an order that still pleased the heart.

5

I had to do a midday report. I played it straight down the line. The crew set me up, X marking the spot, against the background of Cilewent Farmhouse, and I recounted the events: that sweet newsline narrative, in which I pointed this way and that, said that here behind me and there away to my left – in this peaceful setting, I took care to add – this shocking event had occurred. And I wasn't thinking about any of it. I can do that kind of thing in the usual everyday sleep. I was thinking of Pontyrhiw and of how soon I could get up there; of the campaign reports, bulletins and magazines I must look through; all the individual directions which Friedmann would tolerate but with a chronic reluctance, and which he would tolerate at all only if I stood, at stated times, marking the isolated spot, indicating, underlining, making the local history clear enough for transmission. I got the okay back down the line: it was just what they wanted. I had known that.

I was walking back deciding whether to go first to Pontyrhiw or to the bookshops when I got a message that there was to be a press conference. There was a new and important development. The police would receive us at two in the castle. And that was that; I had no choice but to wait. Though it was worth waiting for, in its own odd way. It was Scene Two of this kind of event: the note claiming responsibility.

It had arrived at midday at the office of the Senate. It was in typescript on quarto:

Buxton was shot as a murderer and as an enemy of the people of Britain.

(Signed) *Marcus,*
           Volunteer.

It had been posted before 9 p.m. in central Cardiff. It had been sent for fingerprint testing. But it had also been sent to the photocopier. We had the facsimiles, still stiff with static, in our hands, as if evidence was at last being delivered to us.

The conference was agitated. Superintendent Evans was repeatedly asked if Marcus was known to the police.

'Well it's an unusual name, but we're making all possible inquiries.'

Then attention centred on the significance of the word 'Volunteer'. Did this indicate a member of some secret army? Didn't the word have a sort of military sound? It was too early to say, Evans said, but it was a possibility which they had to bear in mind.

Then what organisations used 'volunteer' as a description of their members?

'Almost all. At least all voluntary organisations,' said a man from Local Broadcasting.

It was mostly like that: a kind of earnest thrashing around. I left before the end and went back to Cardiff. I had decided on the bookshops.

All the tumbling literature was full of the Pontyrhiw shooting and the official inquiry. The editorial lines varied but were mostly united about broadening the scope of the inquiry. Buxton was heavily attacked in all of them, and I supposed from this alone that the groups were already being raided. But only *New Dragon*, the Welsh Left faction of the M-L Alternate, had explicit threats against him: 'An enemy of the people who must be physically brought to account.' They would pay dearly for that phrase, with arrests and raids of their offices, but I didn't take it too seriously. In the competitive situation of the factions in M-L, there is a constant bidding-up of aggressive lines, and I had seen some such phrase about virtually every prominent right-wing politician and trade union leader, as if saying it did some good and might even make it happen.

I was very much more interested in the Gwent Writers' Group pamphlet *Death of a Loader*: a detailed account of the shooting at Pontyrhiw. I had seen extracts from it before, in *Justice*, but this was the full story. I bought it and took it away. I thought I would already know most of the local details, but could read them now from a different point of view; look back at them, in effect, from the Cilewent Farmhouse.

I went to my hotel room. I left my number on call. I am in the habit of reading quickly. Speed reading is adequate for releases. I went at just that speed through the introductory material. The Welsh miners and railwaymen had come on strike together, in early January. But the resulting power shortage hadn't got serious until early March, and Britain was drawing extra supplies from the European grid. Then Wales had reached the limit which the Commission had authorised, and the political pressure shifted again to the power stations. Pontyrhiw was exceptional because it had two months' coal supplies at its No. 1 Depot, which was normally treated as store and reserve. On the second of

March these were ordered to be moved to the generator, at emergency speed including overtime. The miners first, then the railwaymen, appealed for solidarity. The depot met and put on first an overtime ban, then when a loading team was suspended for refusing overtime met again and decided that nothing should be moved. There was a quick change by the management: overtime would not be asked for; the suspended men were reinstated. But the issue had been focused. Another meeting decided to move nothing, until cleared by the miners and the railwaymen. There were two hurried days of appeals and negotiations, then the whole workforce at the depot was dismissed and sent home. In theory, that is to say, for the decision became known and the depot committee decided to stay in and occupy the yard. The police came at once, and stood at all the gates. But the occupation held. Almost all the workers stayed and slept in the depot. The women brought food. Men left only on compassionate grounds, though Gareth Powell, exceptionally, was released to compete in a scrambling trial: he had twice been champion of Gwent. While he was away the army arrived in Pontyrhiw – an infantry company with additional lorries, obviously to take over and move out the coal. But they kept, when they arrived, what they call a low profile (the profile of men with guns is instantly recognisable, all the same, high or low or in the middle). They were awaiting a Government decision; it would be made, it was said, at the highest level. But the situation was urgent: most homes, offices and factories in the district were already cut off from power. On the morning of Thursday the fifteenth of March it appeared that the decision had been taken. The troops moved in to the streets leading down to the depot.

I stopped and shifted my speed. I read it as it came.

6

Extract from *Death of a Loader*

The Pontyrhiw Depot was originally a field beside the Gwent canal, taking direct loads by barge from the neighbouring collieries. The narrow lane by the main gate still led down to the towpath of the disused canal: it had originally been a ferry point. Ferry Road, leading now from Commercial Road to the main gate of the depot, is a double row of working-class cottages, built in the 1870s; their front doors open directly on the narrow pavements. Behind each row is a series of long gardens, on the north running down to the towpath. On the south side the cottages join the high brick wall of the depot. All ordinary movement of coal is by lorry down Ferry Road and along Commercial Road to the power station: a journey of a quarter of a mile. It was this territory that was now in dispute.

There were more than a hundred men in the yard: most of them standing around two great fires of old trestles and planks that had been lit in the loading bays. Gareth Powell, just back, went across to the nearest fire, where he saw several of his friends. There were pans of tea in the edges of the fire, but there were no mugs spare. He was trying to borrow one when an amplified voice filled the yard. All the men turned.

'This is the police. I have an official announcement. By an order made under the powers granted by the State of Emergency, Pontyrhiw No. 1 Power Depot has passed under requisition to the Emergency Supplies Committee, who have instructed a detachment of the security forces to enter the yard and to begin moving the coal which is urgently needed for the restoration of normal supplies of electric power. The detachment will move into the yard at 11.00 hours. All civilian personnel and workforce now present in and around the depot are hereby requested to leave the premises in an orderly fashion, beginning from now. From 10.30 hours onwards, any unauthorised or civilian personnel remaining on the Committee's premises, or in the immediate approaches to the depot, will be breaking the law and will be subject to arrest. Instructions have been given that any such arrests will be at once carried out. It is now 10.08 hours. Will you please begin clearing the area? I repeat, clear the area. Thank you.'

As the amplified voice died away, there were angry shouts from the men around the fires. These continued until Eddie Morgan was seen climbing on top of one of the trucks in the gateway. The men moved over and formed up around him. He lifted his hands for silence.

'Well lads, it's come. They've not just asked us to get out, nor told us to get out. They've ordered us to get out. We'll be arrested if we don't.'

'What you bloody playing at, though?' a voice shouted from the crowd.

'I'm not playing at anything. Nobody's playing any more. This is the showdown, and I'm giving you the facts. I'm also giving you, each and every one of you, this chance to decide. If we stay in the yard, after half-past ten, then we're breaking the law. You heard him say they'll start arresting us. All right: it's your decision. Any man, now, who wants to leave the yard, can come out through the gates and there's no hard feelings.'

'Traitor!' a voice shouted.

'Why give in to the buggers?' shouted another.

'Meanwhile,' Eddie Morgan continued, raising his voice, 'your elected representatives intend to stay in the yard.' There was an immediate cheer. 'And if any of the rest of you want to stay and keep us company, well we can only say you're welcome.'

The cheer which greeted this was loud and sustained. Eddie Morgan waved and got down. The men turned and went back to the fires. It was 10.15.

At 10.25 the police amplifier was heard again. 'This is the police. This is a final announcement. You have five minutes to clear the yard. Five minutes to clear the yard.'

'Your needle's stuck,' somebody shouted back from the gate.

The police amplifier was at the corner of Ferry Road, where it turns into Commercial Road. The officer who was speaking was in uniform and there were several other uniformed men by the car, and two civilians: one of them was the man in the tweed suit who had been at the gates; the other was a grey-haired man in a long dark overcoat. When the announcement had been made, and got only the derisive reply, one of the uniformed men came down to the lines of police at the gates. He passed on an order and the police moved out of line and formed up in a column in Ferry Road. The group of men at the gates watched closely. Most of the reporters went along Ferry Road to the police van, to try to find out what was happening and about to happen. The television crew were already filming.

When the reporters had gone from the gates it was easier to distinguish the people standing there who were not yard workers. Apart from John Davies, who was staying with his union members, there were some twenty people, mostly men. None of these moved when the warning was given. John Davies went over to the one man he knew: Will Prosser, district secretary of the Communist Party.

'You staying, Will? Why?'

'You don't have to ask, John.'

'No, but I am asking. We don't want heroics.'

'No heroics at all. I'm in a public street. Nobody can order me away.'

'They'll get you for obstruction at least.'

'They'd have to prove that.'

'Are these others your people?'

'Some. Half a dozen.'

'And the rest?'

'Phil and Megan over there: they're Trades Council observers. Then our ultra friends.'

'Do you know them?'

'Some. Not all. Half a dozen at least are not from round here.'

'That's what I thought. Anyhow, I just thought I'd say.'

John Davies stepped back and addressed the group. 'It will assist us, I believe, if the only people here are those directly connected with work in the yard.'

'Including yourself?' shouted a young man.

'I've been asked to be here officially, by the men in the yard.'

'Nothing's official any more,' the young man shouted back.

The column of police was called to attention. Everyone looked around. There was nowhere to go but down Ferry Road, where the police were lined up, or along a narrow lane which led round to the side gate of the depot. Otherwise there were only the high yard walls.

The police amplifier sounded again. 'It is now 10.30. You have been given your final warning. Anyone found on the premises of the depot will now be arrested. You can still leave quickly. Anyone walking this way, along Ferry Road and back to the town, will be free to pass.'

'All inside,' Eddie Morgan shouted.

The stewards, and John Davies with them, went back into the yard and stood waiting behind the trucks which were blocking the gate. A whistle was blown, and the police marched towards the gateway. The column was halted a few yards from the trucks. The Chief Inspector nodded. The police started pushing in, along the narrow entry between one truck and the wall. Two of them climbed over to the cabs of the trucks and tried to start the engines to move them, but the motors were dead. Scuffles started along the narrow entry. The police tried to push in, along the narrow entry, but the weight of bodies beyond them was much too heavy: most of the workers had formed up and were solid at the narrow space into the yard. After many shouts and struggles, one man, Mervyn Lewis, was dragged out by the police and passed back into Ferry Road. Two constables led him away.

The struggle in the entry continued, but it was obviously deadlocked. After a few minutes, a whistle sounded again, and the police pulled back: those who had been in the front of the struggle were dishevelled and angry. The Chief Inspector formed them up again in their original lines. There was a loud cheer from the yard and several mocking shouts from the lookers-on, none of whom, at this point, had left.

The Chief Inspector went back to the police van. He talked with the group there for several minutes. John Davies and the stewards had come out again and were watching. The delay dragged on. Other people were now joining the group at the Ferry Road corner,

41

including two army officers. But the centre of the group was the grey-haired man who had been there before. Then there was a new arrival, again in a heavy dark overcoat.

'Christ, you see who that is,' John Davies exclaimed. 'Buxton!' Some of the others also recognised Buxton. Tom Baines laughed.

'Christ, if they can spare a Minister for the Pontyrhiw Depot the country must be easy.'

'No, he's a pushing bugger,' Eddie Morgan said. 'He's into everything himself.'

Buxton was now obviously in charge of the group by the police van. He talked for some minutes, then one of the army officers saluted and doubled away. After another minute, the group dispersed, and the Chief Inspector came back. Then the amplifier sounded again: it was a different voice, but it was not Buxton himself.

'Please listen carefully. You have chosen to break the law. You have resisted lawful arrest. You now have your final chance to come out of the yard. The security forces, in cooperation with the police, have clear orders to enter the yard and to remove anyone or anything that gets in their way. Minimum force will be used, but no opposition or obstruction to the security forces will be tolerated. For your own sakes, you must now clear the yard. You can do nothing to prevent the security forces entering it. You have five minutes.'

The announcement was listened to in silence, and there were no answering shouts when it ended. But it was too late now for any turning back. John Davies went across to the Chief Inspector and talked to him earnestly, asking for more time. The Chief Inspector said that it was out of his hands. John Davies then went on to the police van; the others saw him talking there and being referred from one figure to another. Meanwhile in the yard there was intense activity. Everything within range that could be carried was being stacked behind the trucks that were blocking the gate. The stewards were called back in, and the narrow entry was filled with a stack of the metal trams that were normally used on the depot loading rail. The barricade was completed. It was five minutes to eleven.

There was an interval of stillness and silence: an extraordinary

42

silence. Then, precisely at eleven, the action started. An armoured car drove up fast to the main gateway, making a spectacular stop just short of the barricade. Then it reversed fast, into the lane, so that its guns were covering the main gateway. Once the armoured car was in position the police moved in on the people outside the gate. Those who refused to move were arrested, but there were only three or four; most of them had slipped away down the lane to the towpath. The police then ordered the reporters and the television crew back to the Commercial Road–Ferry Road corner: they went, under protest.

The next phase of the attack then began. An armoured bulldozer had followed the armoured car halfway down Ferry Road. It was now ordered forward, to remove the barricade. At the same time a line of army lorries began moving into Ferry Road from Commercial Road. The leading lorry stopped where the bulldozer had been. There were three men on each lorry, including the driver. The main body of the infantry company was still being held back: this was the policy of minimum force.

The bulldozer approached the barricade and began pushing at it. It was a heavy mass to move, with the jammed trucks, and the bulldozer backed off, to get a different angle, As it was coming forward again, three burning two-gallon oil cans were thrown over the wall, in its path. The whole gateway was shrouded in heavy, acrid black smoke. The bulldozer driver backed off again, away from the smoke. Orders were shouted, and the men from the leading lorries ran forward to clear the cans. They managed to get them clear of the gate area, but when the bulldozer came forward again two more burning cans were thrown, and the black smoke poured out again. The armoured car moved forward a few yards and swung its main gun on the gateway.

Gareth, with several other men, had climbed on a loading bay where they could see over the wall, just down from the gateway. They could just see along Ferry Road to the leading lorry. They could not see clearly who was throwing the cans: it seemed to be some of the younger men, on the other side of the entry. But they saw others running with cans ready to light and throw.

Gareth watched and cheered with the others. Until the actual attack he had felt relatively uninvolved. Like most of the men in

43

the yard he had not really believed it would happen. He now saw the situation, like most of his friends, as a practical problem: no more. He had no doubts whatever about the rightness of what they were doing and he saw the army, if not the police, as aggressors: men brought from outside to intervene, by force, in a local industrial dispute. So the only problems were technical: how to keep them out, how to defend the yard. He would probably not have joined in throwing the burning cans; anyway it had not occurred to him. But as he watched the situation, in its mounting confusion and anger, a plan came to him, and the more he looked at it the more obvious it seemed. The leading lorry had pulled up just short of an alley which broke the row of houses on the south side. It was a narrow alley, between high walls, but it looked just wide enough to get at least the front of the lorry inside. At that angle, the rest of the lorry would then effectively block the street; with the right manoeuvring it could really be jammed. He had seen this happen often, by accident, with delivery lorries. Now it could be done by design and block off the whole street.

He spoke to the man next to him: another loader, Eddie Price. 'If I could get to that front lorry, turn it across the road with its front in that alley, it'd stop the rest coming through.'

'No, mun, never.'

'I tell you I could. Get out the side gate, across into the gardens, then through one of the houses and up into the lorry. I could do it while this lot are clearing the cans.'

'You stay here, mun. Leave it to them.'

'It would hold them up, just that bit. And the more we fight back the more likely it is they'll have second thoughts: pull off and negotiate.'

'Not them, mun. They're trained to it.'

'Well I think it's worth trying.'

'Never.'

'Why not?'

It was in Gareth's whole character to react in this way. In all normal situations he had learned to be cautious, but that was a particular learning, in particular circumstances, like being careful on the road. All his earlier impulses had been quick and active, even reckless, in a young man's way; it was these he had learned to concentrate for the speed, the skills and the quick momentary initiatives of scrambling. It was this kind of instant decision, this seeing and taking a bare but possible chance, that was now uppermost. He could not stay still and watch; he was not a natural spectator. Saying no more to Eddie Price but looking again at the street and counting the houses, he made his practical decision. He climbed down from the bay and ran for the side gate. He still had the key and in a few moments was in the lane. Some of the people who had been outside the gate were still standing there, under the wall, but the armoured car was turned away from them. He relocked the gate and crossed the lane and climbed over the fence of the nearest garden. Somebody shouted to him, but he took no notice. He went on across the gardens, climbing the low intervening fences. He had worked out that he needed to get to the eighth along, and then go through the house to the street. As he ran there was the sound of a minor explosion from behind him: one of the oilcans had burst. He reached the eighth garden and made for the back door. It was through a flimsy lean-to porch, with a wheelbarrow, an old bicycle, a lawnmower, garden tools. He opened the door to the house and called.

An old man came into the passage, in slippers and loose grey cardigan, his stained trousers hanging loosely on his thin body.

'It's all right, mun, don't worry. I work at the depot.'

'What you want?'

'I just want to go through and out your front door.'

'What for? What's happening?'

'The bloody army's attacking the yard.'

'Well I know that. The police come. We was told to keep indoors.'

'Aye, well you do that. I'll just go through.'

There was a woman's voice from the back room.

'She's not well,' the old man said. 'I wanted to get out to ring for the doctor. They said they'd pass the message on.'

'Aye, well it's rough out there now.'

'What you going out for?'

Orders,' Gareth said. The old man nodded. He accepted the word as ending most arguments. 'All right then, thanks,' Gareth said, and pushed past to the front door. The old man watched him as he cautiously opened it and looked out. His judgement of distance had been good; he was within three yards of the leading lorry.

'Right,' Gareth said, and closed the door behind him.

The edges of the smoke were blowing back down the street. There was a crashing noise from the gateway; the bulldozer was pushing the trucks over and in front of it; there was a track beyond it into the yard.

Gareth ran for the cab of the lorry. He was seen at once; there was an angry shout. But he got into the cab. The engine was still warm; it started on the first press of the button. He released the heavy handbrake and got into gear. He had decided to reverse, on a right lock, and then swing back across the road to the left and into the alley. There were running figures of soldiers along the pavement below him; he could see them clearly in the mirror.

'Stop,' came the clear command.

Gareth reversed hard. The clutch was fierce, the lorry jumped back suddenly. There were soldiers now in front of him, and they were lifting their automatics. One of them was holding up an arm to stop.

Gareth changed to forward gear. He swung the big wheel over to a full left lock and released the clutch. The lorry shot across the road, and he had to brake hard as the wall of a house loomed in front of him, while wrestling for maximum lock to get into the alley. As he was braking, he heard the sound of shots. He could not see who was firing. He wanted to reverse again, to get square into the alley. He had got the gear lever back just before he was hit. There was a shout, 'Stop firing,' just as the final shots were fired.

When the first shots had been fired, all movement had stopped at the gateway, except for the continuing noisy wrenching of the bulldozer. It had pulled back from its first angle of clearance and was engaged on a second. Many men from the yard had run forward into the first track and were trying to rebuild the barrier. In the second round of shots, many of these men fell. They were more than twenty yards from the lorry. The firing, it appeared, had not been directed at them. But they lay, hit, in the debris of the gateway. There was a sudden silence.

Then the horn of the lorry started to sound: a long, steady, high

46

wail. The soldiers under it pulled open the door of the cab. Gareth was lying forward over the wheel. He was bleeding heavily from the back.

The bulldozer had now stopped. When the men had fallen in the gateway the driver had at once stopped, then switched off his engine and climbed out. Everyone seemed now to be shouting at once. There were repeated calls for ambulances. The Chief Inspector attempted to take charge.

Gareth lay in the cab, with the horn still wailing. An officer had arrived, from the Commercial Road corner, and after one look had said he must not be moved until an ambulance arrived. But the lorry was still blocking the road. This dictated the sequence. Several men from the yard had now come up to the lorry.

'Who's that up there then?'

'One of your people,' the young officer said, accusingly.

'Bloody madmen. Firing. What you think you're up to?'

'You should ask your own man. He provoked this trouble.'

'It's Gareth,' Eddie Morgan said. He had climbed up and looked at the wounded man in the cab. The blood was soaking the dark back of the coat; there was heavy gasping breathing.

'There's wounded back by the gate,' another man shouted.

'I've sent for stretchermen and ambulances. You must now keep back.'

'Bloody trigger-happy robots,' Eddie Morgan shouted. 'Can't you control your own men?'

'Can't you?' the young officer replied, coldly.

An ambulance had arrived, on the other side of the lorry. Two stretcher-bearers ran round.

'You can't move him till a doctor,' Eddie Morgan warned.

'He has to be moved to get through to the others.'

The horn stopped suddenly. Gareth had slipped sideways, away from the door of the cab. One of the stretcher-bearers climbed up. He put his hands, at arm's length, under Gareth's head, and slowly turned round the face.

'Can he be moved?' the officer called up.

The stretcher-bearer didn't reply.

'Answer me, man. Can he be moved?'

The stretcher-bearer pulled back and looked round. His eyes

47

moved over the whole group who were standing looking up at the cab. 'I'll try', he said. 'Dick, go the other side.'

When the two bearers were in the cab they lifted Gareth gently. They had to support his head, which seemed loose and uncontrolled. The black hair had fallen forward over the white skin. The mouth seemed fixed open, the lips drawn back and blood on the teeth.

'How is he?' asked the officer. He was very pale since he had seen Gareth's face.

'Nothing can be done for him here. Though if we move him...'

'Bring him down,' the officer ordered.

The first bearer climbed down. He arranged the stretcher in the doorway of the cab. He got two men to hold its far end, at the top reach of their arms. Then, pushing and twisting in the crowded cab, he moved Gareth gently back, until his shoulders were on the stretcher. Still twisted in the cab, the two bearers lifted, and the stretcher was pushed forward until it held the whole body. The first bearer came down and slowly, with the other men supporting it, the stretcher was drawn out. Gareth lay with his eyes closed; the noisy breathing had stopped. His coat had fallen open and his grey jersey and blue shirt were soaked with blood. His black singlet showed at the neck as they propped his head with a pillow.

The bearers carried him round to the waiting ambulance. Almost at once it was away, its signal sounding and echoing in the narrow street.

'Weekes, move that lorry. Get it straightened up and close in on the pavement.'

One of the soldiers jumped up and tried to start the engine. The motor whined, but the engine would not start.

'All right, manhandle,' the officer ordered.

The soldiers and the men from the yard began pushing. Weekes stayed in the cab and steered. After two long pushes they had cleared an opening. The police waved two waiting ambulances through.

At the gateway now there was silence. The bulldozer driver was standing with the men from the yard. The crew of the armoured car had got out and were standing looking at the disorder of the overturned trucks and the men lying among them. The police had moved back against the walls of the houses; only three of them were active, guiding the ambulances in.

Eight men had been wounded; they were lying or sitting, attended by their friends. Behind them, in the opened yard, the other men were waiting, standing close together. They were ominously still, watching everything, unwilling to move.

The ambulances were loaded with the wounded men. Five of them, fortunately, were able to walk. The Chief Inspector kept the area clear for them. The young officer who had been at the lorry walked down to see what was happening, but as he came past the ambulances there was a sudden sibilant hissing from the men in the yard. He stopped abruptly, looked round at the armoured car. He seemed to change his mind. He walked across to the armoured car corporal and spoke to him quietly. Then he walked stiffly back up the road, as if he had done what he had come for. The ambulance doors were closed, the lights and signals switched on. They raced away up the street. As they went the crew of the armoured car got back in their vehicle and drove away. The bulldozer driver, seeing them go, went back to his own machine, reversed, and went slowly back up the street. The lorry that Gareth had driven was still stationary on the pavement, but otherwise, within a minute, Ferry Road was empty of vehicles, except for the police van at the Commercial Road corner. The attack had ended.

Gareth died at some point on his way to the hospital: somewhere along the ring road where he had ridden that morning. His wounds had been so severe that there had never, it was said, been any chance of saving his life. The bearers took his body to the hospital; a young Indian doctor confirmed that he was dead.

Of the eight other men wounded, three were in a serious condition and were given priority treatment: John Major, Gwyn Villers, Harry Jones. The five others were treated and kept for observation: Wyndham Davies, Bill Prosser, Tony Prosser, Raymond Pullen, Lewis Jones.

Back at the yard there was a meeting outside the gate, between John Davies, Eddie Morgan and the police Chief Inspector. They were trying to establish what should happen next: the Chief Inspector could only say that he must wait for instructions. But

49

while they were still talking the men in the yard had made their own decision. A crowd of them went to the overturned trucks and set them back on their wheels. They then manoeuvred them back until they again blocked the gateway. But they cleared away the small trams to leave a walking entrance. It was like getting the situation back to just two hours earlier, before anything had happened. Nobody ordered this; it was a collective, almost an instinctive, decision. The lines of police simply watched. It seemed none of their business.

'It looks like they mean it,' the Chief Inspector said to John Davies.

'That's only what I told you.'

'Yes well the point's been made. In the hospital.'

The three men, feeling strangely together, walked up Ferry Road to the abandoned lorry. Two soldiers were standing behind it, on guard. John Davies looked up into the bloodstained cab. The cab door was still open, as if what had happened inside was unfinished.

'What made him do it?' John Davies asked, turning.

'What makes anybody do anything?' Eddie Morgan said angrily.

'Did you know he was trying it?' the Chief Inspector asked.

'No. Of course not. Nobody knew.'

'What was he like then?'

'Gareth? Well, Gareth, he just lived for his bike and for the scrambling. The yard, you see, was only the money for that.'

'Not a militant then?' the Chief Inspector asked.

'What does militant mean?' Eddie Morgan said bitterly. 'Haven't you seen us all?' He gestured back at the gateway.

'No but he did more,' said the Chief Inspector. 'Behind the wall it's different. He stood out and took the risk.'

'Yes,' Eddie said, 'well we know that now.'

'Would you have expected it of him?'

'Expected? Who knows? It's like that in any battle.'

'Not battle,' insisted the Chief Inspector.

'What I don't understand,' John Davies said quietly, 'they must have shot at Gareth from behind the lorry, while he was still moving it. But they'd have shot up, at the cab. So I don't understand how the men were hit by the gate.'

'There'll be an inquiry,' said the Chief Inspector.

'Yes. There will be. Because if you see it from here it couldn't be an accident. They must have fired direct at the gate.'

'I don't know about that. It's too early to say,' said the Chief Inspector.

'And firing at all,' Eddie Morgan insisted. 'That's the real inquiry.'

'You used force to resist,' said the Chief Inspector.

'We defended the yard.'

'And this lorry. Your young fellow seized it.'

'What a thing to do,' Eddie Morgan said, quietly.

'A daft thing.'

'A brave thing.'

'It often comes to the same,' said John Davies, sadly.

The main body of the army detachment was still in place in Commercial Road. They were waiting for further instructions. The Chief Inspector, after checking at the van, took John Davies and Eddie Morgan in his car on a round of the homes of the men who had been hit. As they drove the length of Commercial Road they saw the armed sentries still in place, the lorries lined up, the soldiers standing beside them, talking and smoking. Many people had come out of the houses and were standing at their doorways, talking over what had happened.

They went to Gareth's home first. The police car climbed up the estate roads. A few men had come out to their gateways and watched the police car passing. The sun had come out and was bright on the slopes of the Cefn, where the old bracken had withered to a pale, fine bronze, and the sheep were moving uphill, as always when the weather was clearing. The sunlight caught the bright colours of the paintwork on the neat estate houses: the sharp blues and yellows and greens, the occasional pillar-box red and flaring mauve. By the white paling fences early daffodils and forsythia were flowering; most of the yellow crocuses were tumbled, but the purple and white were still standing: one of the houses had its number, 187, set out in crocus flowers.

'This one on the corner,' Eddie Morgan indicated.

The police car stopped. Eddie and John Davies got out. They went through to the side door and knocked on the glass. It was

51

some time before May came; they had to knock again.

She seemed not to need to be told. Something passed, physically, as she saw them standing there.

'I'm sorry, love, it's Gareth,' Eddie Morgan said quickly. 'He's been hurt, he's at the hospital.'

'Not the bike?'

'No, not the bike. At the depot.'

'Can I go to him?'

'Yes, we got the car.'

She fetched her black raincoat. As she pulled it on Eddie saw that it was duller than her hair. They walked along the entrance.

'Police,' May said, stopping.

'Aye.'

She hesitated. 'Was it fighting at the yard then?'

'No,' Eddie said, and then wondered what he was saying. 'Not like you mean,' he added, lamely.

'I mean them breaking in,' May said, and looked at John Davies.

'Yes, love,' John said.

She buttoned her raincoat and went forward, very stiffly, to the car. She took no notice of the Chief Inspector and the driver as she got in and sat in the back. The car drove down through the estate, watched by more people than when it had come up.

It went fast along the ring road to the hospital and round to the accident reception. John Davies got out with May. Eddie was staying to go on to the other houses.

'How bad is he?' May asked. She seemed released when she was out of the car.

'Pretty bad, love. You must be prepared.'

They went in to the crowded lobby. Other women May knew were there, waiting for news of their husbands or sons. John Davies led the way to the desk.

'Powell? Is that Gareth Powell?' the receptionist asked. She was a tiny woman, with a very thin, ill-tempered face.

'That's right,' John said.

'You're his wife, love, are you?'

'Yes,' May said.

Again something had passed, beyond the words. John Major's

wife, watching her, saw May's body stiffen, as if hit.

'I'll get a nurse, love. I'll have to ask.'

'Where is he?'

The woman looked at John Davies. She couldn't say the mortuary. She had to pass the problem on. But John Davies was slow to pick this up. Ellen Major came over and stood by May.

'Only the doctors are busy with others,' the woman said.

'Not with him,' May said.

The woman looked up at her. There were tears in her narrowed eyes. 'It was too late, love, I'm sorry,' she managed to say.

Ellen Major gripped May's arm and put a hand on her shoulder.

'I still want to see him,' May said,

'Not just yet, love. Wait,' Ellen Major said quietly.

'Why?' May asked, her voice rising.

'Oh the shooting, the bullets,' Ellen Major said, looking at her.

'Bullets!' May screamed. 'What you talking, bullets?'

'It's what it was, love,' Ellen Major said.

May pulled her arm away. She stepped back and looked around. 'You mean they shot him? They shot Gareth? Who shot him?'

'The army,' said Ellen Major, but now John Davies intervened, going forward and taking May's arm.

'It will all be gone into. They won't get away with it.'

'Get away with it? They've shot him,' May shouted. She shook off his hand.

The other women who were waiting had now all got up, and had moved closer to her. John Davies, prepared for grief, saw only anger spreading: an implacable anger that had passed from May to the other women who were waiting.

'We must live with our sadness,' he said, defensively.

They still faced him angrily. He had not expected it. He had expected to comfort, to soothe, but he saw only naked anger, that May's outburst had released.

'Killers,' said one of the older women.

'That's right,' several said.

'It will all be gone into. They won't get away with it,' John Davies repeated.

'Where are they then? What are you doing?' Betty Villers asked angrily.

'They're still down there,' he said. 'There's been enough trouble.'

'Let them come and face us,' Beth Prosser shouted.

John Davies looked around. He was relieved to see a nurse coming through the wards. It was the nurse the receptionist had called.

'Mrs Powell,' she said, calmly, and seemed to pick out May.

'Yes.'

She turned to lead the way, through a side exit. May turned and followed her. The others hesitated, then Ellen Major went after her. There was a brief silence and then the women gathered around John Davies, questioning him intently.

May followed the nurse along the glass-covered walk. Their heels were loud on the tiles of the walk. The wind cut across through the openings from the yard.

The nurse stopped at the mortuary door. She looked quickly at May's face. May stared back at her. She was now very pale. Her hair had sprung loose. She put up a hand to touch it. Ellen Major stayed close.

'This way then, Mrs Powell.'

They went into the cold of the mortuary. Gareth was lying on a table under the skylight, a brown sheet draped over him. The nurse pulled back the sheet from the head. May gasped. His face was so steady, so peaceful: it was not what she had looked for. The skin was pale and tightly drawn, but the fine curling hair was so beautifully in place that he seemed more like a figure or a photograph than an actual man. May stared down at him, then leaned over and kissed his cheek. As she drew slowly back the nurse was standing ready to replace the sheet. But May moved suddenly, and gripped the sheet. She pulled it back from his chest and then stiffened, holding the sheet. There was livid dark bruising and the dark holes of bullet wounds on his left breast, on his side, on his shoulders. The nurse tried to recover the sheet, but slowly, looking down, May pulled the sheet back, until the whole body was uncovered.

Below the waist he was untouched: the thick black hair undisturbed against the smooth pale skin. Ellen Major had her arm round May's waist. They both looked down at him, silently. The

54

young nurse also waited, looking steadily at the body.

May put out her hand and gently touched the bruising and wounds. Then she moved and bent over and kissed his lips. She turned, still holding the sheet, leaving the body uncovered. She handed the sheet to the nurse. She walked out with Ellen Major.

7

I found myself out in the street. I was walking steadily along the pavement, with people moving around me, and I did not know how I had got there; I had no memory at all of leaving my room and coming down in the lift. As I began to notice my surroundings I felt only a sense of displacement. It was as if I was moving in two ways, two places, at once.

I eventually remembered what I was supposed to be thinking about. It was not Pontyrhiw, which, by Insatel standards, was dead; only Buxton was alive. I recalled a telecast reference: 'The riot at Pontyrhiw, in which, it will be remembered' (because it is not remembered) 'there were casualties, one of them fatal.' But presumably I am employed because I can make connections. Friedmann knows this in theory, and from past cases, but in every new one he forgets it. So I knew what he knew I should be doing.

I went back to the hotel room. I kept an eye on the screens. Already there were identikit pictures of the young man in the cap, with reproductions of the note from 'Marcus, Volunteer'. Most of the pictures were already labelled Marcus, and there was a free range on Volunteers, with not a fact in sight.

My own thoughts still moved in another direction. Of the hundreds of words in that Pontyrhiw pamphlet, only six now stuck, as I got back to my job: 'The television crew were already filming.' I had seen nothing of Pontyrhiw when it happened. I had been in Italy on one of Friedmann's more improbable hunches. And there was no film of the attack itself. As the pamphlet said, the crew had been moved before it began. But what interested me more now was the group outside the gates, the unofficial group. There might well, in passing, be film of them.

I got on to the Insatel library. I dialled a line and got what film there was played through. It looked different from the pamphlet but it didn't contradict it. I froze several frames of the group outside the gates. It was a very long shot, but suddenly I froze in my turn. Standing among the group, not prominently but, as I stopped it, quite visibly, was a bearded young man in a blue denim cap. He was between two girls: one tall and fair, one shorter and very dark. Then someone walked across, and they were gone from sight again.

I stared at the frames for some minutes. Then I started checking to get the names of the crew. One of them, Carl Howard, I had occasionally worked with. It took three calls to get him, but I would have made three hundred. I kept it professional. I was working, I told him, on the Pontyrhiw inquiry; I'd been checking back through the film.

'You know they moved us out, Lewis?'

'Yeah.'

'So it's only atmosphere stuff. If we could have got the army...'

'Yeah.'

'But they were taking no chances. They didn't want it on film.'

'Yeah. Too bad. Still I thought I'd ask. In case you'd seen any more.'

'Not a chance, Lewis. They closed us right down.'

'Yeah. Too bad. And before that, I suppose, the strikers

weren't exactly cooperative?'

'A bit of this, a bit of that. Mostly the media as the class enemy.'

'Yeah. Silly buggers.'

'Right.'

'And the hangers on, outside?'

'Oh as usual, worse. The usual politicals.'

'Yeah, Rentamob. And I'm still trying to trace witnesses. I've got most of them pinned but there's a man and two girls, they don't look local.'

'No. Though wait a minute, a blonde. What was she called? Lucy. That I remember.'

'The blonde.'

'Well, of course, but she was okay. It was the woman with her. Christ, yes. She really went for us, semi-professionally. She must have been reading some paperback or something.'

'Sure.'

'She asked why we were filming from what she called the police side. If we wanted the action they would let us in the yard. We could film as the army came in.'

'Christ!'

'Right. A real nut. Rosa. Rosa something. She'd got hold of some jargon. She might even have worked somewhere.'

'I know the type. Okay. There'll be nothing useful from them. And this guy with them? With a beard, a black beard?'

'Oh him, yes. Looking tough and saying nothing. It was this Rosa character did all the talking.'

'She actually wanted you to go in the yard?'

'More than that, Lewis. Into the actual barricade. She said it would be a historic moment.'

'Well it would have, actually. Newsfilm of the year.'

'Sure, Lewis. Don't think I've not thought that. But it was

so obviously not on.'

'Yeah, well. One way or the other they all keep us out.'

'Right. But luck anyway.'

'Thanks, Carl. Luck.'

And luck I supposed it was. But I would have to play it carefully. Very carefully indeed. I'd even wait a while before getting prints of the frames. What mattered, above all, was that I should be asking the questions. I didn't want them occurring to anybody else.

So I would go the long way round. Now I knew what to ask about I would follow up on the pamphlet. For what it disclosed but didn't disclose was that its author or authors had probably been in that group at the gate. The narrative was general and what they call impersonal, but it assumed close presence: perhaps as the usual convention, more probably as fact.

That made it next stop the Gwent Writers' Group. Past that title, too, there would be some actual author or authors. I had some difficulty getting their secretary's address. I finally got it through the Arts Board. I rang her: a Mrs Rees. She sounded simple, but she would give me nothing. It was Group policy, she said, not to publicise the names of individual contributory authors. I told her how much I'd admired the account, and how I might get parts of it into Insatel, with full credit to the Group. She said she would welcome this, but that any offer must be made to the Group as a body. I said that of course I understood this, but that preliminary discussion with the actual authors, about the parts that might be used or adapted, would in any case be necessary, for obvious technical reasons. She said that she was sorry; she would take any details I might care to give her, and pass on any messages, but I would understand she had no authority to vary the policy of the Group: 'however attractive the offer', she was sweet enough to add.

I did it the hard way. I went to the Central Library and got out all the Group's bulletins. It isn't an organisation with secret membership, of course; all the members were listed there, as they joined. But after allowing for resignations there were still over ninety. That's how many writers we all have these days, and Gwent, clearly, is no exception.

It was useless trying to do much. I rang a few names at random, and all the names from the immediate vicinity of Pontyrhiw. But I either got the same answer or, more often, no answer at all; several members of the group who had been on the demonstration had in fact, I learned later, been detained for questioning. I noted some names to compare with the eventual police lists, but that would inevitably take time. In some of the later calls, I changed my approach and said I was a writer wanting to join the Group; my kind of work, I said, was very close to things like *Death of a Loader,* and I was particularly interested in working with people like the authors of that. I got nothing. Ten years, even five years ago, it would certainly have worked: almost everyone, then, talked openly, uncautiously, as if a random question was always exactly what it seemed. Not now, evidently. I even got one blasting: after being told to send the Secretary my name and address and some samples of my work, when I persisted I was told to piss off back to my typewriter; he had work to do if I hadn't.

I walked away from that whistling happily: thanking whoever I could think of (there weren't that many, to whom that kind of thanks could be properly addressed) that there were still, somehow, a few human beings around. But then there was nothing for it but to go back to the castle. As soon as I arrived I picked up the excitement: there had been another discovery. I was in time to make the press conference, and all was revealed: a second orange mountain cape had been found, during a search by the staff, on the southern edge of the park.

Several reporters, as soon as they heard of it, went off to file their stories: *Evidence of Second Assassin*; *The Second Man*. Most of us stayed to watch Superintendent Evans perform. He was very good. He pointed out that the second cape might be unconnected with the shooting. He touched it and said: 'This is a common article in our tourist localities.' Then, when nobody believed him, and since he clearly didn't believe it himself, there was some genuinely interesting discussion. What he actually believed, obviously, was the second man version: one to throw the smoke bombs, one to come out with the shotgun. In all probability it was the assailant's cape that had first been discovered, on the path beyond the sheep pens behind the farmhouse, and this second cape belonged to the smoke-bomber, who had taken a different escape route.

I watched and listened. I didn't know either way but I remembered the account of the museum guide Jones, who had been closest to the man with the gun and who had insisted that he had run off to the west and away from the farmhouse. If he was right – and who was more likely to be? – there would still, of course, be two men, but with their roles and escape routes reversed. But as I looked at Evans's big map this seemed more and more improbable. Indeed, from the map, it looked crazy for anyone to have tried to escape in the direction in which the second cape was found.

This was now being discussed in the conference. The Superintendent agreed that to escape that way meant

61

crossing, in effect, the whole area of the Open Museum. Most of the crossing, it was true, was in the cover of woodland, but he had also to cross at least four main paths, on any of which he might easily have been seen. This was reasonably persuasive, though what nobody was saying was that the entire park had been cleared for the Buxton visit. On any ordinary summer evening all that area he was supposed to have run through, and the paths he crossed, would have been crowded with visitors. On this evening, for the sake of security, another and unlooked-for security had been arranged, for the assailant. If he could succeed, in the first moments, in drawing the search behind the farmhouse, he had a large empty area to escape through. And had he not in fact succeeded in exactly this, with everyone except Evans? There would then be no reason to suppose a second man at all: the cape on the path behind the farmhouse could have been put there, beforehand, to mislead and draw off the pursuit.

Of course once you get into this kind of speculation, there is literally no end to it. The second cape might also have been planted, but then for what reason? The cape actually worn had to be got rid of, but while the first served some purpose the second, so far as I could see, didn't; it was more probably a genuine disposal, before he got out of the park and risked being found with it. Either way what came through, even more strongly than from the original account of the attack, was a sense of extraordinary coolness, self-possession, courage if that word is still allowed to be used in such unpopular contexts. And of course a coolness backed up by meticulous planning: there had never been any real doubt of that. You could also add other details: the conference was rapidly doing so, still on the assumption of a second man. To take the long escape route, even with the advantage of the park being empty, suggested someone very fit as well as very confident: a long run like that wouldn't be lightly undertaken, under the risk of probable or even possible pursuit.

So the portraits were emerging, but it was just these portraits, of one man or two, that really, I thought, should provoke reflection. And especially of course the first. It was so obvious, when you thought about it, that the young man with the shotgun had dressed in ways to make sure he would be remembered: remembered, that is, at the level of what he showed. Who in their senses, otherwise, would wear an orange mountain cape – a garment especially designed for long-distance recognition – to carry out a dangerous attack? And on a fine summer evening, with most people in shirt sleeves! It was then worth thinking about the smoke-bombs, and especially about the second. The first smoke, obviously, was cover for the attack, but wasn't the second, really, to cover the start of the long escape route: the cover he had to have to mislead the pursuit? And if that was so there was no need at all to imagine a second man. It could be a single operation, but then one with a very marked character: a character that might lead us to some more authentic portrait.

For what was really coming through was a special kind of calculation, with these steps. First, that *he meant to be seen, in a recognisable and memorable form.* Another way to put this is that he meant not to be seen, as himself, at all. Second, that *like the clothes the attack was blatant.* He could have shot from cover; he chose to shoot in the open, facing his target. He could, from seven yards, have shot to kill or to wound more seriously; he chose, surely deliberately, to

63

shoot at the legs. Third, *he wanted to come face to face with Buxton, and he wanted Buxton to see his attacker*. He wanted, you could say, the drama of that moment in which it was obvious that the gun would be fired: not drama as gesture, a self-regarding pose, but drama as a moment of significant public action. Put these features together and what did you get? Not the assassination attempt that the rest of the media were screaming about, but something different, however rough: *an attack that was primarily a form of demonstration*.

I didn't share these thoughts at the conference. I didn't want its largely synthetic indignation redirected at me, but in any case I wanted the real solution, and I wanted it on my own. I joined in only to ask about Buxton; of course respectfully. He was making good progress, Superintendent Evans reported. All the shots, fortunately, had hit well below the knee. In fact, Evans added, most of the shot from the two barrels had hit the grass just in front of where the Minister was standing; the police had recovered it from the turf. Obviously, Evans added, the assailant had shot very low, in the excitement of the moment, and we could all be thankful that he had. And as I heard this admirable sentiment, capping the news I had hoped for about the (as I assumed, deliberate) direction of the shot, I pencilled in a fourth feature of the assailant's portrait, a feature that all along had been insistently suggesting itself: that he had *techniques to get others to see things in ways he wanted them to see them*. It was becoming a possible portrait, and of course my mind went back to Pontyrhiw: to the young man in the cap, and the two girls with him: Lucy and Rosa; the argument with the television crew. An argument about position, about point of view.

I went around Cardiff that evening, looking up old friends, old contacts, wondering if the words were still interchangeable. Everyone I met had a story of being questioned or of a friend being raided, and so of course they watched what they were saying. But it was a firm opinion, and a general one, that nobody local was involved. I still didn't know, and the Welsh can be very persuasive. I brought names into the conversations from time to time, but I got no response to Rosa and Lucy. In the end it was just a way of filling in the evening.

I arranged to go back to London next day, but only after the reconstruction, which the police had announced, at the conference, for seven in the morning. I thought this would at any rate be sufficiently bizarre.

They did it very well. They had matches for Buxton and his party, walking up through the park and its relics. The rest of us were standing at some distance from the farmhouse, mostly joking, but when the first smoke bomb went off we all jumped and it was chilling for a moment when the young man stepped out with the shotgun and fired his blanks. They had dressed the young constable well: all the publicised features stood out remarkably: the blue cap, the orange cape, the dark glasses, the long fair hair and beard. Perhaps it was just the effect of the staging, with two men with stopwatches timing every movement, but my own reaction, after the initial shock, was the corroding scepticism I am so often accused of. It just didn't add up, as a real event. It was so clearly a presentation. Indeed everyone, suddenly, began talking about disguise. The man next to me said: 'Take off the cap and the cape and the dark glasses, and what have you got: any young man with fair hair and a beard.' But that, as a magician will tell you, is the secret of any disguise: you see through what you are looking at, what you are meant to be looking at, while the real disguise escapes you. Even the few who took the improbable next step – 'perhaps the hair and the beard were false too' – still saw, beyond it, only the fixed if now shadowy figure of a young man. I myself didn't know what other figure to look for, but I confirmed my belief that none of us, any longer, knew who we were looking for, even in general terms: the staged reconstruction was of an initially staged event.

The police, meanwhile, had their own things to do. The whole sequence was repeated, with special attention to the timings and distances of the smoke bombs. Then two young officers were set to run, in different directions – one along the path behind the farmhouse, where the first cape was found; one through cover and down through the park; we lost sight of him quite quickly. After a long wait they came back with timings. It was all good amateur acting, but it meant very little. I stayed to the end, and looked in on the subsequent conference, where there was a fine technical presentation of all the timings and distances. But my mind was on something quite different, and I went back to settle my hotel bill and to get to the airport. (Friedmann's jet had of course gone back. He would have had a total identity crisis if deprived of it any longer.) But I now knew what I was looking for. I would get back to London and do a little updated study of the radical theatre.

8

I was prevented by a further discovery. This came through while I was actually leaving the hotel: a tip phoned through by a friendly colleague. The police had found a car: *the* car. It was the first real evidence, I then thought, that had not been set up for discovery. It had been found, in Llandaff, by the most ordinary police inquiry routines. Somebody, while everything else was being done, had set up the normal procedure of checking all reports of stolen or abandoned vehicles. Most of these led nowhere, though there had been some temporary excitement, not publicised at the time, about a stolen car found in the airport car park; this turned out to be unconnected. The real car went undetected longer: mainly because it had been parked, quite normally, in a street near Llandaff Cathedral where most of the residents normally park in the road. I wondered, when I heard this, if it was part of what I had guessed as the pattern, but everything I imagined was an underestimate, as indeed it had been throughout.

In a street like that a car might stand for days without really being noticed; everyone assumes that it belongs to someone else. But with the special instruction in force, one experienced constable got interested in it, inquiring at all the neighbouring houses. When he drew a blank he reported the number, for routine check, and it turned out to belong to a car-hire firm – Rentaday Motors – in South London. There might still have been no immediate action, but when the hire firm was asked who had rented it they gave the name J. Tiller, a young man in his middle twenties who had said he was a German student touring Britain; he had mentioned to the girl in the office that he was especially looking forward to visiting Wales. This really started things up. The combination of young man and German and student and Wales was of course irresistible. Every house in the street was called on, but 'nobody like that' (it's an exact phrase) lived or had been seen there. Then the car was searched and of course – for by now I was certain – a blue denim cap was found pushed under the front seat: 'in the haste of his getaway,' one of the agency reporters filed.

I saw no evidence of haste. On the contrary, this trail of planted clues was becoming embarrassing. Indeed I only got really interested when I heard, from the police, that 'J. Tiller' had given a London address and that it was not false. I used my plane ticket but I was still well behind them; they withheld the address for six hours, to make sure of their search. But then they let in the press, for it was what everyone had been looking for: a stage set, in effect, of a young revolutionary's 'hideout'. There were the portraits of Marx and of Lenin, the posters from Iran and Bolivia and the Yemen, the calendar from China, the bookcases full of revolutionary classics and pamphlets. I had seen scores of such rooms: they vary very little except for some small idiosyncrasy of private decoration or ornament and a few personal photographs. What now struck me at once was the fullness of the stereotype and what seemed, at first sight, the total absence of even the smallest idiosyncrasy, including the absence of any personal papers or letters, or even names on the fly-leaves of books. There was a comfortable bed, a cheap table and four chairs, and the standard portraits and posters and books: you could almost read the stage manager's list.

I said nothing about this. The police and most of the reporters were so clearly satisfied. Was there any further information about J. Tiller? 'Not as of this time.' No neighbour (why didn't they say, to be accurate, adjacent occupant?) remembered seeing him. On two occasions the rent had been paid, in cash, by a girl. It was now two months overdue, the landlord had been trying to make contact or to regain possession. Slowly, on the spot, the marvellous lead ran out. So I went off to my news piece: I played it straight, as everyone else was reporting it.

But I guessed, correctly, what was really happening. The computer would already be running for Tiller: any Tiller who had ever been in the country would be checked on Gridfile, which had become operational during the previous year. They would announce its results when they were ready.

They announced nothing for several days. In fact, as they admitted later, they had got what they wanted within an hour: not indeed a J. Tiller, but from their point of view even better, a Marcus Tiller, born in 1959 at Duisburg in the German Federal Republic, student of law in Marburg, graduate student in the University of California 1984–86, entered Britain December 1986, in which month the room had been rented. There was only one problem: Marcus Tiller had left Britain in March 1987, and there was no record of his re-entry. The announcement was delayed because the police then concluded that he had come back at some time before early July and might be still in the country. All departure points were secretly warned. They seemed still to expect, several days after the shooting, that they would quietly pick him up. Incidentally, from his Gridfile photograph, he had long fair hair but no beard. He had been officially (unofficially) photographed twice again, on demonstrations in the December and the February; in each case with no beard. But that seemed no problem. Nothing seemed a problem, except picking him up. Of course they contacted the German Federal police, in case he had got out earlier. The Germans reported a long record of political militancy, including four arrests and two convictions for obstruction and assault. He was not now at any of the addresses which they had for him.

So there it was: the case seemed solved. It only remained to find Marcus Tiller. After three days without success, they released his photograph: the newspapers and television carried it prominently: *Marcus the Volunteer*; *Red Marcus*; *The Hunt for Marcus*; *Where is Marcus?* It was only a matter of time before he would be found and charged.

I kept in touch with all this, naturally, and let my own reports follow it, but I doubted every word. The trail was so obviously planted. It didn't make sense that the skill of the actual operation could coexist with this unbelievable sequence of carelessness. On the contrary, everything fitted an alternative explanation: that the entire programme had been carefully set up; that the police, at each stage, were being carefully misdirected by their own stereotypes; that things were set out for them to find which it was known they would be looking for; that every move, in fact, was part of an elaborate distraction and disguise. But if that were true, one fact emerged which it would be safe to rely on: a fact about the character of the individual or the group who had conceived it.

It is often said, with conventional certainty, that radical groups and individuals are humourless: this is part of the ordinary model of fanaticism. It is quite often true, but no more than anywhere else: certainly no more, say, than in official politics. Yet even when it is allowed that, privately and often publicly, these people enjoy jokes and games with the next man, still, in this case, there was an unusual feature. The whole thing was too sustained, too elaborate, to be reduced to the normal bursts of high-spirited hoaxing and mockery. And when you put this beside the real act at the centre of it – even though Buxton was now making good progress and could look forward to complete eventual recovery – you got another kind of mind: the cold pleasure of the game of deception, the probably collaborative wit of the insistent false trails, had somewhere inside them an unusually hard edge: a certain settled bitterness; what I thought of, indeed, as an older kind of bitterness.

But that left me baffled. I kept sticking on one point. After all this was a game, if I was right, not only with the police – the fair game – but with the unfortunate Marcus Tiller, now being looked for across half Europe. And what could be the reason for that? A split or a personal quarrel? Neither seemed enough of a reason; neither, in any case, could be an excuse. Then what exactly? A quite different dimension began to suggest itself.

While I was thinking this through I went on trying to get information about Rosa and Lucy and the man with them. It took longer than I expected; I was now too well known as working for Insatel. But I made it, eventually, on a personal ticket: a lover's search for a tall blonde.

'Lucy Peele perhaps? She used to be around.'

'It was after a party. I only got as far as Lucy.'

'It sounds far enough.'

From there it didn't take long: just a few phone calls. She was living in Highgate with a man called Bill Chaney; they weren't there, though; they were in Ireland, caravanning. In fact, as I discovered when I went and watched their flat in Highgate, they were back; just back, I found out from the postman. I went on watching. Three people lived there: Lucy, who was really very beautiful – anybody who had seen her would understand my interest and my questions; all they wouldn't understand was ever losing touch with her; Bill Chaney, middle-height, dark-bearded, with strong glasses; and a second girl, middle-height, very black shining hair, big eyes, creamy skin. She and Bill were most often together, going in and out. Lucy, who evidently had some regular job, going in and out at fairly fixed hours, was much more often on her own, although in the evenings all three sometimes went out together.

The second girl was obviously Rosa. I got the phone number and called and asked for Rosa.

'Who wants her?' It sounded like Lucy. 'A friend of a friend.' That used to be a password; it had evidently become obsolete.

'What name?'

'Lewis. Lewis Redfern.'

A pause, a fragment of speech in the distance.

'She isn't here.'

A sharp ring-off.

She was there of course. I had seen her go in. I wondered what to do next, but she solved that for me. She came out soon after, with a suitcase, and walked to the tube. I followed her. She went to Baron's Court. She walked to 43 Mount Pleasant and went up in the lift to the third floor. I checked the postboxes. On the third floor there was a name I recognised: Mark Evans. The real case began.

PART TWO

1

Edmund Buxton and Mark Evans. It seemed an impossible connection, along the track I was following. Of course they had once been connected. Back in the seventies they were both junior ministers in a Labour government (that name takes you back). In their middle forties, and therefore (by public standards) coming men, they usually seemed indistinguishable, in that massive appearance of consensus which is called government. Most of us blocked them, and confused them, with a score of others: tribunes in business suits, technicians of percentages and cost–benefit analyses, who would occasionally disconcert us by raising, from some far recess of their vocabulary, words like equality and compassion and even socialism. The Sunday talk of busy men. A discourse of surplus values.

If the committed among us then made a distinction between them, it was to despise Evans more. For Buxton had always been a functionary, while Evans had once been a political thinker. And we had seen a lot like him: the humane or radical book, the year or two of radical campaigning, as career steps to the suit and the office and a life of administered power. Mark Evans, I remember a friend saying, was 'a very bad boyo: one of the pack of metropolitan Welshmen with enough radical gas to inflate any expense account'. So we laughed when he got beaten in 1981: lost his seat, as they say, in the unmusical chairs which has become the standard political game; different from the old parlour game because chairs are *added* in each round, as this extraordinary bureaucracy – State, business, media, academic – expands. Even then, with added chairs, so many of these wax men want to play that the occasional individual has to drop out. Goodbye, Mark Evans, and thank you.

There's just one thing, though, about unmusical chairs. New and elegant variations are continually being devised. Thus, when Evans reissued his book, *The Limits of Representative Democracy*, which had once meant a lot to us before we saw him living and loving the limits, a whole new sequence began. A few cynics thought they saw it: a predictable step in the career cycle. Most of these career politicians make a bid for intellectual or even political respectability when they are out of office, so that they can go back in on a higher rung. And anyway they need the money.

The Evans sequence was more subtle, and the irony is that we in the opposition – the well-known 'extremists' of the long-running 'lunatic fringe' – were a necessary part of it. Thinking to capitalise on disillusion with 'parliamentary politics', we began using Evans's book. That harshly critical new preface, on his parliamentary and ministerial experience, gave us so many exact quotes. Then, almost imperceptibly, another process started happening, through widening bands of the naive and the hopeful: 'Evans himself admits' became 'Evans points out' and then 'as Mark Evans shows'. The 'guilty con-man' became 'the repentant villain' and, before too long, 'the man with enough honesty to learn from his mistakes'. From there it was only a step to a new radical authority, 'one of our leading radical thinkers'.

I paid no special attention to Evans. The whole process

was finishing me. It's great to belong to a young radical generation, until you have to watch them grow up. There were innumerable examples, much nearer to hand than these clapped-out petty theorists and out-of-office functionaries. Buxton, of course, was simpler. He took a seat on the board of International Electronics, in his 'scientific and technical capacity'. Evans, however, became Director of the American-funded Community Politics Trust: a liberal rat-trap, if ever there was one, picking up young radicals just when they needed a settled income; the voluntary work of a decade becoming funded and incorporated, along impeccably liberal lines. But it completed his reconstitution as hero. He had money, he gave grants. Thus he was a man worth knowing and, when you got to know him, was basically very decent. So by the time of the Coalition Government Buxton and Evans could be contrasted: Buxton in his resumed political career, which led him without regret to the attack on the workers at Pontyrhiw; Evans on the respectable radical fringe, supporting social projects and experiments in a score of cities and towns. They still seemed to me, when I thought of them, different local eddies in the same historical stream. If you accepted its directions, you could reasonably contrast them, but essentially, I thought, they were the same kind of man.

Was I wrong, I now had to ask? Or was it simple coincidence that the trail from Pontyrhiw had led, improbably, to Mark Evans's flat? I stared for some time at the postbox, then went away to find a phone and make a few simple checks. Evans, Mark was listed at that address in the phone directory. I rang the number. A woman answered, perhaps Rosa. I explained, genially, that I was from Times-Europe: we were thinking of a series on the Community Politics

Trust, so could I speak to Mr Evans?

'You've surely tried his office?' It was a very cool, putting down voice.

'He seemed not to be there,' I said. 'They gave me his home number. After a little persuasion.'

'I really don't see how that could have happened. They know quite well that he's abroad.'

'Oh, gosh. Is that Mrs Evans?'

'Does that matter?'

'It would to some. But I'm sorry to have missed him. Do you happen to know when he'll be back?'

'No, I can't help you. You had better try his office.'

But I had all I wanted. She could stay points North. Ms Glacier.

Yet what, after all, did I have? It was all very vague: my phone call to Rosa followed by her leaving her flat with a suitcase and ending up at Mark Evans's. There could be twenty other reasons for that. And would someone leave again, after this other call? I watched for an hour, but nobody left. I decided to take it the long way round.

I called the Trust Offices, sticking to Times-Europe in case Ms Glacier checked. I got a warm voice this time: selected by interview to sound like Community Politics. Yes indeed, Mr Evans was abroad. She was so sorry, perhaps someone else could help. Well yes he was in Zambia, that was the conference, but he was probably going on to Mauritius: there was a working party. It was a shame I had missed him, he would have been so glad to talk to me. No, he'd left on the tenth. Yes, that was really bad luck.

July tenth. The day after the Buxton shooting. Was that luck or judgement? But it was still no use as a thread. I had to research Evans properly, though I was still not sure why

I was really doing it. Yet I research careers rather often. They have a certain morbid interest, even when they lead to nothing in particular.

Ms Glacier was still a pain in the back, and I scratched that way as soon as I saw his divorce. But it had been nothing much: more like a career step. His first wife, obviously a friend from college, had petitioned after twenty-one years. There had been two sons of the marriage, David and Evan. Its end was now five years back. The other woman mentioned in the petition was a Louise Praager, an art dealer. Evans had apparently lived, more or less regularly, in her flat in London for two years before the divorce. His wife, a teacher, was at their home in Wales, in what had been his constituency. He had once been MP for Ewyas; his country address had been Llanmawnog Hall (Llanmawnog Hall – the limits of representative democracy!).

I followed it up: she was still there, Mrs Joan Evans, still a teacher, in a sixth-form college. Then I backtracked on Evans himself. Before he became an MP he had been a Labour college organiser. His book had come out in 1965, and in 1966 he got a job as Deputy Director of the Extra-Mural Department in the University of Wales at Brecon. In 1968 he was made Director and moved to Llanmawnog Hall; in 1970 he was elected to Parliament. The rest I knew.

It was a steady pattern: Mrs Praager in London, Mrs Evans in Wales. Parliamentary and Ministerial duties; the long sessions; the shortening constituency visits and vacations. Nothing unusual about that. Nothing unusual, either, that Mrs Praager, at the time of the divorce, was forty-seven, exactly the same age as Evans. Nothing flighty about it; just a steady alternative relationship. But they didn't marry after the divorce was through. Perhaps Mrs

Praager, also, had an alternative relationship; I mean other than her original one. 1984 the new edition of his book; 1985 Director of the newly formed Community Politics Trust. (From book to director, twice in a career; that showed perseverance.) Then 1986 married Sarah Brant, twenty-four. Nothing unusual about that either.

I moved on to Somerset House. It is full, these days, of young women inventing genealogies for alienated Americans. They have a professional air which makes casual research seem intrusive. A few old ladies were looking for birth certificates for their pensions. Odd scholars were still hoping to find some writer's bastard. It didn't take me very long: the more recent volumes don't interest any of these. The third quarterly volume: Brant, Sarah. I put in a form for the birth certificate and while I was waiting tried *Who's Who*. It saved more searching: Brant, Sir Martin John, Professor of Medicine, University of London; widower; wife d. 1965 (such a little letter, d. for deceased); two d. (this time daughters): Sarah, b. 1962, Rosamund, b. 1964. My Rosa, I presumed.

I got the birth certificates anyway, and the marriage certificate for the elder daughter and Evans. It all checked as foreseen. I had a drink on it. I was still only playing a hunch, but I had been right so far. The Rosa who had been at Pontyrhiw was the sister-in-law of Mark Evans. Evans had gone abroad the day after Buxton's shooting. Rosa had gone to her sister's straight after my call. And she and Lucy Peele and Bill Chaney had been in Ireland, had they, when Buxton got shot? That deserved a little look.

I was walking away, thinking it all through, when I suddenly got very depressed. It wasn't just the drink, which always does that to me. Nor was it only that other irresistible sense of intrusion. I make inquiries like this all the time. I believe in my job as an investigative reporter: far too much is hidden in this kind of society; far too few connections are traced and followed through. Yet at times, of course, I look at myself, when something irrelevant jolts the research sequence and I have knowledge of someone which I know I don't need and which would undoubtedly embarrass or hurt him. I usually burn it, but forgetting it isn't so easy. You meet someone and you know this about him and you're very careful not to know it; it's common form in this kind of society.

These passing depressions were there, but it was something else, and then I knew what it was. I had a lead, certainly, but it was mostly supposition. Was I really telling myself, even just as hypothesis, that Mark Evans was involved, however indirectly, in the attack on Buxton? Certainly I had sensed, in the planning, some older and harsher mind. But Evans? Everything suggested he was soft – full of good intentions, humane insights and genial impulses: the combination is standard in his kind of limited and conscience-stricken collaboration. And no real motive surely. Perhaps he had hated Buxton, but that wouldn't be enough. In that world they play out their hatred in talk.

Then another thought struck me: the Welsh connection. I went and looked at a map. Nothing much from that: fifty miles between Pontyrhiw and Llanmawnog Hall, between an industrial valley and the green border farms. No real connection there. But I looked up Evans again in *Who's Who*. Son of Joshua Evans and Ruth Evans (*née* Lewis). These bloody Welsh names aren't enough to go round, and they so often tack on the Hebrew bits: the Jews of Britain. But I went back to Somerset House and got his birth certificate: Joshua

Evans, lorry driver; Ruth Evans, *née* Lewis; place of birth, Cwmdu. Back to the map, and a jump of interest: Cwmdu is a village eight miles from Pontyrhiw. I got the parents' ages from the certificate and tracked back for a marriage certificate. That took a long time; I could only guess how long it might have taken to conceive him. Just over four years as it turned out. Joshua and Ruth were married in 1930. I ordered their certificate and got my next break: Ruth, when she got married, was Ruth Davies, widow. I settled down and tracked her back. It took a long time. The young women legitimising assorted Americans came almost, I think, to take me for a colleague. Then I got it, in 1919: Ruth Lewis, spinster, married Thomas Davies, miner, at Cwmdu. Back then to the succession of cumbersome volumes, births quarter by quarter, from 1920. I found it in January–March, 1923. John Thomas Davies, son of Thomas and Ruth.

So Mark Evans had a half-brother. It would be worth looking out for him. But my eyes had been seeing Davieses for five hours solid: how the hell would I ever find this one? I tried *Who's Who* and then *Who Was Who*: three John Thomas Davieses, but not this one; all different parents.

I gave up. I went back to see what the police might be offering. It was still the first days of the public advertisement of Marcus Tiller. In spite of my doubts I felt I had better switch to that, keeping this other in reserve. Then as I was going down in a lift I remembered *Death of a Loader*: the union official who had been there that morning when the army attacked: John Davies. I rang union headquarters, to get his full name and address. They got it from the files: John Thomas Davies, 8 Station Road, Cwmdu.

2

I rang John Davies. I told him I was working on the Pontyrhiw Inquiry. We saw eye to eye on that. Then I got the information I needed by mentioning, in passing, that I was in touch with his half-brother, Mark Evans.

'Yes,' he said, 'my brother. He's been helping us on the Memorial.' The Memorial, I sorted out, was what they were calling their campaign.

'You still need this support from outside?'

'Mark isn't outside. But yes, we need support.'

'He told me,' I said. 'In fact he put me on to it. But unfortunately, now, it's got much more difficult. Since this shooting of Buxton.'

He paused before he answered. 'We don't see how that affects it,' he said.

'No, not the real issue. But you know how it is. These bosses in the media.'

'You ought to get them to listen to Mark. He told us something like that would happen.'

'He told you Buxton would get shot?'

'Not that part. How could he? But he could see the situation.'

'When was this, Mr Davies?'

'Well, from the beginning. But he made it very clear at the Memorial that weekend.'

'Which weekend?'

'The one he was down here. The one before the shooting.'

I held on to the phone. I had somehow to manage my voice. 'Yes, now I remember. I was trying to get him that Monday.'

'He went back to London the Monday. He had to go to Africa.'

I couldn't push it any more. I had to spend the next ten minutes on talk about the Inquiry. I even got interested, though it was mostly dull, procedural stuff. But now I really had what I wanted: Mark Evans in Wales while Buxton was being shot.

My shred of a hunch, my improbable hypothesis, seemed to be gathering evidence at an extraordinary rate. Perhaps there was even something wrong, and it was coming together too easily. In this case, from the beginning, the most obvious thing about evidence was that it had been put there to be found. Yet I'd got on to this by so circuitous a route, by a set of indications still so basically improbable, that I felt I could waive the caution, or at least that I could make the next obvious moves. There was no easy way that I could check when Mark Evans had caught the train to London, on that crucial Monday. But I could try his office, and then I could try his wife.

His office couldn't help, though they tried. I had switched back to Insatel and to my own name. I was researching a telebiography, there were facts I wanted to check. But although they confirmed that he'd been in Wales that weekend, they couldn't help about the Monday, and I couldn't ask too directly. He'd not been in the office on the Monday, that was all I could get, from a circuitous question involving some other quite mythical appointment. But it didn't help. Buxton had been shot at half-past seven in the evening. What mattered now was an exact train time, and they clearly couldn't give it me. I checked the timetable. From eight o'clock on there were three trains to London: he could have taken any of them, but equally, by then, he could already have been back in London, being surprised, if not shocked, by the news of the attack.

So I had no option: I had to try the big one. I had to call on Mrs Evans, Sarah Brant. And when I called on the one Brant I might call on the other. Rosa, Rosamund, could still be staying with her sister.

I got my personal assistant to arrange an appointment. The more impersonal it sounded the better. The telebiography was still the come-on, and I covered my tracks by putting in a memo outlining it, in case somebody checked. Celia said Mrs Evans sounded pleased. Not Ms Glacier. Not for a telebiography.

She was alone in the flat when I arrived. She had got up from working at a big oval mahogany table by the wide south window. The flat was opulent. I suppose in her style. I had no idea what Mark Evans's furnishing style, if any, might be. The chairs and sofa in the drawing room were covered in gold and crimson silks; the curtains were a heavy gold brocade. Then porcelain and silver and rosewood and walnut and again mahogany. Mrs Evans suited them all.

She was younger than me but felt older. She will last for twenty years quite as well as her furniture: in a steady deep gloss. When age begins to show its first stains and scratches they will still, for another twenty years, be absorbed in the patina of a lifetime's care. Flesh can do this much, if it is really cosseted, and of this there was every sign. Her hand was quite cold as it touched mine, the fingers loose for a second, the opal ring very large, registering a momentary shape.

Rosa, when I had seen her in sweater and jeans, had the same shining black hair, the plump creamy skin, the large, clear, dark eyes. But Rosa was still a girl, her movements impulsive, often awkward, her expressions uncalculated though by custom rather hard and challenging; a girl with a girl's grievances. Sarah, Mrs Mark Evans, was only two years older but was an epoch different: wholly composed, deeply confident and satisfied: an efficient continuity of body and what serves for mind. I looked at her table while she was talking. Her first remarks, inevitably, were all about people she knew in my world: a member of the Board; a senior producer; a research engineer, but perhaps I wasn't 'bothered with the hard stuff'; three writers – there are always plenty of *them*. She had a lovely cornflower-blue file, if you can call a paper-holder of that elegance by such a short, hard name. Three good pens of different colours were arranged beside it. Beside her chair, which had a deep cushion, was a heavy leather briefcase; the initials M.E. An expensive recorder had its trailing microphone by the curled edge of the drapes.

'I'm doing an edition of Mark's essays,' she said, following my eyes to the table. 'We shall bring it out in the spring.'

'We?'

'I've gone back to Warren, Steinberg: I was an editor with them before I married Mark.'

'You gave up work when you married?'

She seemed momentarily disconcerted.

'We travelled a lot together. At first, especially, Mark liked having me with him.'

'But not now?' I wanted to ask. 'Has his doctor told him to give up cream for a season?'

She noticed my hesitation, though I supposed she couldn't

interpret it. She made the obvious transition. She loved working; she had wanted to get back to it. And of course she had been Mark's editor, at Warren, Steinberg, when he had reissued *LRD*. I translated *LRD*. *The Limits of Representative Democracy* had no kind of resonance in that particular setting.

Mark's editor: the description was appropriate. I could see the smooth affair, the smooth marriage. I had been prepared to meet, if not exactly a child bride, at least a girl, a young woman, with some freshness and vulnerability, who had married, been married by, this much older, successful man. I had cast her as the simple, admiring object of one of those ritual renewals of executive vigour which his class goes in for; it doesn't last but it can start like that. Not with Mark's editor! He would have been cut, proofread and indexed so politely and so fast that he'd be a paperback husband in no time: of course a successful paperback husband.

'Is there enough for a new book?' I asked with the Campari.

'He doesn't think so. But then he's very exacting. And he has this big thing planned. It will be something quite major.'

'May I be told?'

'Of course, though we must clear it with him if you want to refer to it. It's *The End of Social Democracy*.'

'Yes, that would be major.'

'It's not finished, that's the point. And I don't want him to hurry it. It's more important to get it right. And then, from a publishing point of view, this book of essays is perfect. It keeps his name current and gives him a breathing space for the big one.'

She was now getting seriously on my nerves. I wanted to

get to my real questions, but she was so smooth and gracious I couldn't resist trying to rile her. 'What would that be, exactly? "The end of social democracy." Do you mean updated late Weber or in effect the Red Guards?'

'You mean what does Mark mean,' she corrected me smoothly. 'Well neither of those.' That put them in their place. 'What he foresees,' she continued, 'is the end of politics, taking politics as we know it, representative politics, which means alienated forms of decision. In the recovery of direct decision-making, which is going to be possible with the new communications, a whole stifling political tradition will come to an end.'

'I see,' I remarked.

It was a very long way from the shooting of Buxton. It was even further from Insatel, where the new communications were happening. But I could play this pat-ball with the larger possibilities. I'd had plenty of practice. We used to do it all the time.

It was then half an hour before we got back to earth. All I wanted to know, after all, was the time of a train. But get anyone on to the end of social democracy and it's a fact that they'll never get up in the morning. Like the Russian revolutionaries of Chekhov's period: they sat up all night bringing their social wills to bear (it's called raising consciousness) and then of course had to sleep all next day while the people went on suffering. Mark Evans! Exactly! I'd seen his reference to that, in his famous preface. That is the destiny, he had said, of some generations, and we should learn to honour them; they are a necessary preparation. They also serve who only sit up and talk.

I got her back, eventually, though I had to go to Wales to do it. I threw in the bit about the Welsh sense of community.

You would expect this new thinking, I said, to come from a Welshman. And Mark was still a Welshman, wasn't he? He still often went down there.

She liked that. It was good image-building. She could probably already see it there in the blurb. Anyway she was much more receptive when I got to the point.

'Actually someone told me he was down there just before he went to Zambia.'

'Yes, the weekend. At the Pontyrhiw Memorial.'

'That was the weekend before Edmund Buxton got shot. How did Mark react to that?'

'It upset him.'

'When you told him?'

'No, he knew.'

'On the train or something?'

'I don't know. He just knew. He got in very late.'

'And he was upset?'

'Very upset. He didn't sleep for hours.'

'Did he say anything?'

She touched the sky-blue folder. 'You don't know him, you said, Mr Redfern. But at times like that he can get very Welsh: very emotional, almost biblical. Of course he said it was madly provocative. Even Buxton, he said, should have had more sense. But it was more than that. He said it was desperately shocking. It was a pattern of violence he had been trying to make clear, trying to warn was coming. The sins of the fathers, I remember him saying.'

'The sins of the fathers? Buxton is hardly the next generation.'

'No, but what he was meaning was the inheritance, you see. The way a pattern gets established and then can only deepen.'

'But then no shock, surely, if you have seen it coming?'

'It was still bad the next morning. He wanted to cancel his trip. He said he couldn't think of going now that this had happened.'

'But of course he had to?'

'Well, it was all arranged. It's an important conference. All the different organisations in community politics. Some of the Africans, you know, are especially far on.'

'So he had to control his feelings.'

'Well, yes. Though not altogether. He actually said, while I was packing his bags: "This is the nonsense I've got into: going half across the world on community politics while my own community is under attack and under suspicion."'

'And so you finished packing his bags.'

'Yes,' she said, and gave me a really beautiful smile.

I now wanted only to leave. I eased myself to take-off by getting details of when he'd be back, which I wanted anyway, and from there to a date for a planning meeting, about the telebiography. She enjoyed every moment of this: dates, times, places, a delightfully ordered life. So I could then get out on a wave of satisfaction: our business well done. It was only as I was leaving that I asked my last question.

'By the way I know your sister, I think. Rosa?'

'Rosie? Yes, I expect so. She used to be with Channel Five.'

'That's it. I was wondering where. Is she still in London? I haven't seen her for some time.'

'Oh yes. She's freelancing now.'

I appeared to make a note. Freelancing, indeed, would be a new word for it.

'Do you see her often?'

'Oh, yes, she comes over.'

I nodded. I held out my hand. She let me take her hand very firmly. I had become a colleague. And anyway it wouldn't mark her, even the print wouldn't show. She saw me to the door. I could get in touch again whenever I wanted, though that wasn't the phrase used: 'whenever you want more about Mark'. Like everything else about her, that was exactly right.

3

I now had a great deal to think about and a great deal to do. But I was again interrupted by what happened about Tiller. What happened, in fact, was that he was suddenly dropped. You need to be inside the media to notice, easily, that kind of negative signal, but of course when you are it's child's play. For days they'd been running Tiller's photograph, interviewing people, hashing it up to the last stringy fragments. And they would have gone on doing that, for another week at least. Or some of them would have: *I knew Marcus Tiller*; *Jet Set Terrorists*; *Marcus and the Death List*: at least one more weekend of that. Then it all stopped, suddenly and simultaneously. Not a word anywhere. That meant only one thing: the bar had been slammed down. I went to the office and got this confirmed, but of course that was only the start. What I had now to get was the reason.

It took a couple of days' hard digging, meaning talking and getting through a really extraordinary amount of alcohol. But of course I got it in the end; several of us did, putting two and two together by familiar rules. The real point was that Tiller had been found. He was in South Africa. He had been there since May: via Germany and Spain after he had left England. He couldn't possibly have come back to England in late June, when the car was rented, or in July when Buxton was shot. In fact he had been at a conference, in Johannesburg, while it was all happening. So, end of that trail.

But the end of the trail wasn't the reason for the silence. We didn't then get the full details but somebody, clearly, had been given the word on Tiller. Not only was he not the young man in the blue denim cap or the young man who had rented the Llandaff car. He was even more evidently not a German revolutionary student. In Germany, in California, in England, he had been doing something quite different. I could take it fairly easily from there, though I didn't get back past a certain point. All that was certain, but it was quite enough, was that at some point in his political activity in Germany – perhaps from the very beginning, certainly from 1983 onwards – he became an undercover staff man in PRC (Political Research and Consultancy), which looks after the deep political penetration of left-wing and radical movements.

PRC, of course, has a quite open and straight existence, with headquarters in Amsterdam. It publishes, by subscription, bulletins and special studies on the political situation and political movements in Western Europe and North America. It has links with Social Research Consultants (Africa), which has headquarters in Monrovia, and with Social and Political Consultancy (Asia), which has headquarters in Singapore. The main clients of these services are banks, international companies and industrial corporations; the subscriptions are high. Since 1982 we have known that PRC certainly, and perhaps its associates, maintains also a Special Service, which provides information not only on national political underground movements but especially – and here it has become the leading organisation in its field – on international links between these kinds of movement.

93

The money to fund this work has diverse and often untraceable sources: one of the earliest sources, it has been established, was a conference of several international airlines, in the period of hijacking in the mid-seventies. Other sources almost certainly include governments.

One of PRC's established methods, and a principal reason for its success, is recruitment from the edges of the political underground itself. Most national and official security organisations still recruit, by habit, from more safe and orthodox young men and women, who then assume (as if they were drug squad members) superficial characteristics of the subculture they wish to penetrate. PRC, in general, goes for the real thing. And when it has a recruit it does not keep him long in his own country: usually no more than a year, during which he is not only allowed but encouraged to be an active or even leading militant. If he is arrested and fined or imprisoned he takes his punishment, like anyone else. But the main point is to get contacts, where necessary backed up by a record, for his first real assignment, which will be in another country. International student and youth exchange schemes are used wherever possible. So he arrives in his new country with an orthodox reason and an appropriate political record. He can then move, quite quickly, into the investigation of international links; there have been at least three cases in which PRC men have actually carried vital planning and contact information.

Thus, by the time he went as a graduate student to California, Tiller was certainly a PRC agent. Indeed a warning about him was passed but seems to have failed to get through; the real international contacts between revolutionary and radical movements are much more haphazard and inefficient than their surveyors suppose. From the length of his stay in England – only four months – it seems probable that he had no primary assignment but was following a link from California which included some English element.

It seems probable that while he was in England the warning about him eventually got through. It is as well to be unspecific about these matters, but it has been taken for granted, since the role of PRC became known in 1982, that the obvious counter-measure, of volunteers from the radical movements to penetrate PRC, has been put into effect. Certainly in the course of 1985 several names of PRC men were discreetly circulated. The resulting atmosphere is of course quite dreadful. The penetrators and the counter-penetrators exist: nobody can laugh them off as a conspiratorial fantasy. At the same time, as in some of the worst of the past, this dimension gets invoked in factional disputes and organisational disagreements which are quite internal and natural to the movements concerned. Yet it is really something to be able to say, of a man who disagrees with you, that he is PRC: not so much to his face as quietly and discreetly, to your mutual friends. Many good people have been sickened by the endemic suspicion and the casual slander that are then natural consequences, but at the same time they know there are still good reasons for vigilance.

The word that Tiller was PRC seems to have been passed by February 1987 at latest. His departure in March, and his reassignment to so distant a field as South Africa, suggests, also, that this was known to PRC. What mattered to me was that he was sufficiently identified, by some people in England, to be available as a set-up suspect for the St Fagans operation. The elaborate and bitter joke of the car-hiring and the note signed Marcus, Volunteer must have been set in motion by at latest mid-June. Somebody must have been very sure about him, although this is an area in which real certainty, as opposed to strong and effective suspicion, is understandably quite rare. That narrowed the field quite a lot, and I had no hesitation about my own next move. I must trace Tiller's contacts back, until I found some intersection with the lines from Pontyrhiw and St Fagans. Moreover, because of Tiller's flat in London, I could disregard, perhaps permanently, the Welsh connection.

Could I also disregard the line to Mark Evans? I was very reluctant to do this. For complicated reasons, and some not so complicated, he was, to put it crudely, a more satisfying enemy than anyone else I could conceive. His whole style sickened me, and if I had to define it I would point, simply, to his success in his double role, a role that only a few of us seemed to see as double: his success in the world, in that familiar kind of conscience-stricken collaboration; his paradoxical success in the margins of that world, as a genuine radical authority.

I spent some time thinking about the Community Politics Trust, which Evans directed. It is American-funded, as I have said. Its possible links with PRC, which for its own reasons often finances such bland ventures, would certainly need to be looked for. I set up some preliminary inquiries, in the States, but these would take time.

Meanwhile I had more immediate business. Tiller's rent, I remembered, had been paid by a girl. 'Tiller's car had been hired by a young man. The police could hardly hope to do that kind of tracing: the available field was too large. Moreover they were clearly embarrassed by the turn of events about Tiller. I don't know how much they had been told, but that the media got so quick a notice to lay off suggested some efficient contact between PRC and the authorities. So the police, now, were unlikely to be doing much more about him. I was in a different position. I had three people – one young man, two girls – whom I could at once try.

That afternoon and evening I got photographs of Bill, Rosa and Lucy: quite easily, on doorsteps, from my car. The next morning I went down to the hire-firm, Rentaday. They looked at my photographs, and very carefully at the photograph of Bill. But no, they were quite certain: it had not been him. It wasn't easy to remember, but the girl who had filled in the form remembered a fair-haired, tall, rather handsome young man; well-spoken, she added, whatever that may mean. I went in to the rent office: an estate agency covering for a property company (South-Western Metropolitan Holdings). I spoke to an older woman, rather sharp and still resentful about the unpaid rent. I showed Rosa's photograph first. No, nothing like her. Then Lucy's photograph. A pause, a careful look, further scrutiny under the light. Then yes, certainly: this was the girl who had come in, twice, to pay Mr Tiller's rent.

4

That was good news and bad news. Of course I knew very little about any of them, but at least from casual observation I had friendly feelings about Lucy, and I don't mean only that I found her attractive.

It was a triple deck at that flat in Highgate: Rosa had now moved back. But although I had been told that Lucy was living with Bill Chaney, this wasn't what I saw. The other two were always together, and if Lucy was there she was just tagging after them. Again neither of the others had a regular job, but Lucy both worked and, so far as I had seen, did most of the shopping. I was probably only extrapolating from various situations I remembered, but I thought I recognised the pattern. For a year or two, on the fringe, you are all in the same situation: some of you have jobs, some don't, and it isn't important: regular jobs are just bourgeois hang-ups, and if you don't find work that suits you, as you feel at the moment, there's always the SS (we all called Social Security the SS). And the same with somewhere to live. Property, again, is a bourgeois hang-up: all you really need is a room or a bed, so if somebody has one, and is paying the rent, you don't argue about it, you stay for a while and then you offer to chip in.

It's a way of life, and it works for short periods. But if you stay in it long you get to know about people, and you only delay what you're getting to know if you insist on calling it bourgeois. The rows that eventually blow up are spectacular, often mixed up, of course, with political and intellectual disagreements, and as often with changes of partner. What's really interesting, though, is that they're surprisingly often about money, especially for medium-term things like electricity or telephone bills, where the amounts required are beyond the weekly kitty or the agreed weekly rent and food. One of my own friends had a theory that the most fruitful time for really radical theoretical divergences was when the phone bill arrived.

Within such situations there are also, inevitably, victims: more practical, more committed, more faithful, more simple. 'They enjoy it', the others say; 'that's their hang-up', whether it's trying to do repairs or clean up the kitchen or keep an income. 'Natural fodder for bourgeois society', and of course that's right: ragged-trousered philanthropists, patched-jeans philanthropists: providing some minimal base for the more comfortable, more assured though often locally very disturbed upper-middle-class kids, or the truly careless and indifferent from anywhere.

I knew about Rosa, and I had the advantage of knowing her comfortable sister. Bill Chaney I couldn't get: he might have been anything, but the situation was familiar: he was living with Lucy but taking Rosa out. And if any of this was right that left Lucy in the middle, in every way.

We got talking quite easily. I followed her to work, which was at a nursery school in Tottenham. I went back for the afternoon release, when a crowd of parents were getting their children back. I hung on through the first rush and then went to the porch. She was on her knees putting sandals on an extraordinarily sullen small boy. This was made more difficult by the fact that as she put each sandal

99

on, the small boy promptly eased it off again. She was wearing a bright green smock. Her hair was falling over her face. When she heard my step she looked up and smiled.

'You must be John's father,' she said, with some relief.

'Do I look like it?'

She frowned. 'Well, aren't you?'

'No. Sorry.'

'Who, then? All the others have gone.'

'Is this John?'

'Yes.'

'Why don't you let him walk in his socks? Wouldn't that impress on him the importance of shoes?'

'It could,' she said, still harassed. 'But then he might go home without them and I doubt...'

'Surely his mother or father...'

'I've never seen his father. That's why I thought it was you. And his mother's often late.'

'From the office?'

'No. Washing up after some pigs in a West End hotel.'

'If I was really his father I'd rescue her from that.'

'Would you?' she said.

She stood up. John had found a new occupation: staring open-mouthed at me. For all I knew I was about to be claimed. But I had more to be aware of. Lucy was standing quite close to me. She was indeed very beautiful. But what I was actually getting was the hardest, plainest, most direct stare I've ever had in my life. I've seen others being looked at like that, but not to their faces: across the room, obliquely, at a meeting or a party, or as someone turns away. But this was straight at me. It was so intent that it seemed to turn her face to marble. The skin was noticeably paler with the effort of concentration. The eyes – well I thought of all the metallic images and got some notion of how they were first conceived. But no emotion was implied: it was simply extraordinarily attentive, and I can only say, flatly, that I'd never seen anything like it.

I didn't have to answer her question. It was being answered for me, and I didn't particularly want to know what the answer was. Fortunately, just then, a woman arrived: John's mother. I'd been expecting, from the work, some broken-down, middle-aged victim. This was a smart, busty, flamboyant woman in her early thirties.

As soon as he saw her John again kicked off his sandals. She went straight over to him, hit him very hard on the back, shoved the sandals back on and pulled. He was out and away, crying, before Lucy or I really got what was happening.

'Do they all do that?' I risked asking.

'Of course not.'

'Don't you disapprove? When you've just been pouring your kindness into the sand?'

'I do nothing of the sort. She has to look after him.'

'Like that?'

'Any way she can.'

She moved away, tidying up. She took off her green overall. She got her handbag. She stopped when she saw that I was still there. 'Did you come to make an inquiry?' she asked politely.

'You could put it like that. I'm a friend of a friend.'

'About putting a child in the school?'

'No, Lucy. I got to you through Harry Young.'

'Got to me?'

'Yes, I wanted to talk to you.'

She was wearing a pink shirt and grey jeans. She shook

her hair loose of the shirt collar. She fastened its top button. 'You must excuse me,' she said, and began to walk past me. She had assumed, easily, an acquired social mode. God knows how many times, looking as she did, she had had to brush men off.

'I wouldn't have taken this trouble,' I said, 'if it hadn't been so important.'

'Really.'

The tone was cold. 'If I can reassure you, this isn't a pick-up.'

'You're right,' she said.

'My name's Lewis Redfern. We have lots of friends in common.'

She stopped and glanced at me. We were out in the yard. The sun was shining into the asphalt. 'You rang up and asked for Rosa?'

'Yes. You said she wasn't in.'

She blushed, then recovered. 'What do you want then?'

'To talk to you.'

'No, thank you,' she said, and walked off across the yard.

'Lucy,' I called.

She didn't look back.

'You remember Marcus Tiller?'

She stopped, involuntarily. It was a moment or two before she again hurried on. I ran and caught her up.

'Will you go away?' she said, pathetically, as I fell in step beside her.

'I'm a friend, Lucy. You may not think so, but I'm a friend. And I'm probably the one person in London, outside your immediate circle, who knows you used to live with Marcus Tiller.' She kept a brave set face. She kept walking. 'Marcus Tiller,' I went on, 'a man the police and the papers

102

have been screaming about. Screaming for information. Wanting help in their inquiries.'

'I don't bother with papers,' she said.

'You must still have heard.'

She turned and faced me. 'I've got nothing to say to you.'

I smiled. I got out the photograph of her I had taken in Highgate. I held it out to her. She glanced down at it and then tore it up, clenching the bits in her fist.

'The estate office remembered you. You paid his rent.'

'I know nothing about it,' she said, staring at me. But it wasn't the earlier searching stare. She was now obviously frightened. Her denial was an honest person's poor attempt at a lie.

'Have you worked long at the nursery school?' I asked, to break the tension.

'A year,' she said.

'Is that always your kind of work?'

'No. I used to be a model.'

'I'm not surprised,' I said gallantly. She looked across at me as if I was making her sick. 'Why did you give it up?'

'It was pathetic,' she said sharply.

'Then why did you do it?'

'I thought it would be great. I was in a shop in Chester. I hit out for London. I got all the breaks.'

'Good for you.'

'I said breaks. I meant breaks.'

'Men annoyed you,' I suggested. 'You got tired of being a cross between a coat hanger and a sex object.'

'I learned a few things.'

'And then met a few people. Found a different perspective.'

'As a matter of fact, yes.'

'Rosa and Bill? Harry Young's commune? Marcus Tiller?' She was again staring. I pushed my advantage. 'Where no men annoyed you, nobody treated you as a sex object?'

She was blushing again. She should really have stayed in Chester. 'Who are you?' she made an effort to ask.

'I said, Lewis Redfern.'

'What do you do?'

'I'm a reporter. With Insatel.'

She took a deep breath. Then she nodded. 'On the hunt for Marcus?'

'More or less. Mostly more.'

She came to a decision; she was now extremely frightened. 'I've got nothing to tell you.'

'Except that you lived with him.'

'I did *not* live with him.'

'I've been there, love. It's a very small flat. One table, one bed.'

'You're filthy,' she said.

It took me by surprise. As she spoke she turned away and hurried along to a bus stop. I could have caught her up and gone on with the questions. But I didn't manage it. I had no real need, I would get nothing else from her, but it was more than that. I'm used to hard words, it's my trade. But 'filthy', just like that; just a quiet, ordinary word in the street, from this vulnerable girl with her pink shirt and her long yellow hair. It wasn't easy to take.

But now I did tremble for her. She would get the breaks again.

5

My own next moves were obvious but I didn't get to them straightaway. I was sure I had begun to unravel a fairly complicated plot but I had also, with a certain phoney assurance, got myself, as investigator, into almost as complicated a position. Up to my last two moves everything I had done had been indirect, satisfyingly indirect. But the identification of Lucy's photograph at the estate office could well have crossed more direct inquiries. If the woman told the police, they might follow it up, even if they were officially off Tiller; they might even, eventually, trace it to me and then possibly – that indeed would be a direct question – to Lucy. Again, I had declared my real interest to Lucy: given my own name, and Insatel, and the hunt for Tiller. If, or really when, she told her friends Bill and Rosa, it might not be long before Rosa talked to her sister, who would of course identify me in quite another capacity. If either of these things happened, you could say the fat would be in the fire. But I wasn't saying it. It's a common phrase for trouble but put it another way round, the fat makes the fire burn more brightly. It's all a question, really, of the actual operation you're engaged in.

I didn't fail to notice the fact that my two direct moves had been in connection with Lucy. I picked up the obvious explanation, turned it over once or twice, but then didn't buy it. At some point, after all, I would have had to come into the open, and make direct moves. It was just a question of when.

I thought I had better ring Friedmann. When we're put on a story we're given plenty of rope, but at the public level this story was dying, and he wasn't the kind of man who'd want a respectful account of the funeral. I was delayed in getting through to him, and when I did he sounded quite breathlessly executive, but then he's practised that. What was more interesting, after the first few phrases, was that he seemed hardly to know who I was. I concluded that he must, for once, have been genuinely busy. By Insatel standards, anyway, the Buxton shooting was now in its turn an old, rather local affair. With Tiller excluded the police were back to routine and the media were back to where the fires burned brightest: the fighting in Bolivia, an aircrash over the ice, a walkout in Brussels. When he eventually managed to get me in focus he told me to come back: there was plenty to do, God knows he said twice. I said I needed three days: it could be a big one. He had a call coming through, or he sounded as if he had. When I repeated the request, to make certain, he gave the impression that he'd already agreed to it, so I didn't waste time arguing; I went off to dig in my field.

I took a plane to Cardiff and hired a car. I was looking for a reporter who had been at Pontyrhiw. I found one, at the Inquiry, which was still dragging on: a young man, Bleddyn Rees, from the *Gwent Argus*. After some preliminary chat I got out my photographs of Lucy and Rosa and Bill. I was after eye-witnesses, I carefully explained. I'd been told about these three, but I hadn't yet traced them. Had he happened to see any of them at the gate that morning? He wasn't sure about Bill, though there had been a young man. But the girls, certainly, especially the tall blonde. I had to swerve

106

like a rugby player to avoid being nudged. Who were they anyway? Well, as I'd said, people I was trying to trace, for my background piece on the Inquiry. 'Witnesses of that morning's brutal events?' He said 'brutal' with the conventionally indignant Welsh vowel. We parted amicably. And that was Lucy double-checked at Pontyrhiw.

I still hesitated about Ireland: my obvious next move. It would be long and boring; it might in any case be pointless. But if Bill and Rosa and Lucy were really involved at St Fagans – all I had got so far, except the link with Tiller, was the connection to Pontyrhiw – their story about Ireland had to be taken apart. I hung around for some time, then on an impulse, really, I drove up to Pontyrhiw. I had never been there, though it had become so significant.

I drove over the black top from Cwmdu. I got steadily more depressed. The road was so neat, so lined and signed, so macadamed and whitewashed, over that empty hill. I looked at the line of spruce along the reservoir, in the valley below; at the black barren tips climbing out of the sour bracken; at the lines of houses, at odd angles, so bare and exposed, each row seeming to finish in nothing, as if it had been merely interrupted. Then below me, suddenly, were the slate roofs of Pontyrhiw; the grey arc of the bypass, the red houses spreading up the farther hillside, the great concrete towers of the generating station. An industrial area, but South Wales is more than that. What really got through to me was the stark contiguity of the otherwise empty landscape – the bare and barren hills – with this crowded, dirty, unfinished and abandoned development. The people had to live between two inadequate worlds, each harsh and unspectacular: simply a raw transition, within which, unbelievably, there was the talk, perhaps the practice, of community.

107

I found my way down to Commercial Road and then Ferry Road, the names confirming the grey huddled houses, the tickover shops, the sudden garish modernisation of garages and showrooms. There in front of me was the gate of the depot; it had been repaired but it was still firmly locked. No work had been done in that yard since the shooting; the coal stocks inside had been tactfully forgotten. Some of the pits were still out; the men had found jobs elsewhere. The men from the depot were working, most of them, in other yards. The strike had not stayed solid, but it had not collapsed either. The situation had drifted into a familiar pattern: in part accommodation, the wages taken; in part disintegration and run down.

I got out and walked around. There were bullet marks ringed in fading chalk on the walls of two houses. There was a heavy oil stain in the road, where Gareth's lorry must have stood. I walked down past the gate and the depot wall to the canal bank. I noticed the side gate and the fence marking Gareth's route: they were now so ordinary, so neglected, that I had to stare to make them significant. The canal bank was empty except for a man fishing, by his motorbike, along towards the bridge. I stared into the water: it was grey but not obviously polluted; just a little surface debris. That seemed the style in Pontyrhiw.

I walked back and turned the car. I drove back along Gareth's route from his home: the traffic lights, the ring road, the hill up to the estate. I had his address in the file; I stopped and checked it. It was a house among the others: again nothing special. By the white paling fence there was an overgrown hedge of yellow musk roses. The scent was strong. I got out and looked around: at the view of the hill, with the sheep and the dense green bracken; at the tidy houses, with people working in their gardens and cleaning their cars. All this was at an absolute distance from the events I had been following, but the connections, though hidden, seemed real.

I opened the decorative gate. I walked down the side of the house. A woman and a child were sitting on a patch of lawn by the shed. The woman was mending a skirt, the child was sitting watching her. I might have turned away but the child looked up and noticed me.

'Mam, there's a man.'

Mrs Powell looked up. I was not prepared for her. The face was reddened by the sun, the nose prominent. The black hair stood out in a great springing mane; it had just been washed, obviously, and she had not pinned or tied it back; it was loose and wild. I would have said, just looking at her, Greek or southern Italian. She wore a tight, black, satiny dress.

'Yes?'

The voice was so harsh that it checked me. A quick aggression: no look of a victim, yet she had been a victim.

'I'm sorry to disturb you,' I managed to say. I felt weak and stupid. I had no business in that garden.

She got up, folding the skirt. 'What is it you want, then?'

If I could have answered that! But all the drive, all the energy, had left me. Even the habit of contact had left me. Since I had come over the top, and seen Pontyrhiw, I had been feeling quite different: a dazed sadness, a loss of normal continuity.

'Mrs Powell?' I said. There was nothing else.

'Yes. What you want?'

It was so hard and sharp I couldn't quite believe it. I was obviously carrying some wrong model in my mind.

109

'I'm sorry, I'm reporting the Inquiry, I'm trying to get the whole background.'

'Why sorry?'

'I only meant, I'm sorry if I'm intruding.'

'Then why intrude?'

'We all want to get at the truth, don't we?'

She stared me straight in the face. 'We all know the truth here.'

'Yes, of course, as a personal tragedy.'

'That's what you call it. You don't have to give it names. I know it. This child knows it. If you're a reporter go where there's something to report.'

'It's easy to forget what it all really means.'

'No it's not,' she said.

She was still looking straight at me. I don't know what she would have looked like, before her husband's death, or now, if she arranged herself. But there was nothing of that: only the raw face and the loose hair. It came through as ugly: this bitter rejection of outsiders.

There was a noise behind me, and I turned. A young man was coming in past the shed. What struck me at once, as I took in his appearance, was his resemblance to the photographs I had seen of Gareth. A pleasant-looking, healthy young man: square-faced, reddish-skinned, with dark curly hair. He was wearing a scarlet sports shirt and very light blue jeans. He was smiling as he came to us, already calling to the child. Then he stopped. He looked between us.

'May?'

'Bob.'

'Who's this then?'

'Some reporter.'

'Do you want him?'

'No.'

She turned away and bent to her daughter. Bob took a step towards me.

'All right, mister, you heard.'

'Are you Mrs Powell's...'

'Brother. All right?'

'Well yes. And look, I'm sorry about this, but I...'

'You heard. Out.'

He jerked his thumb towards the road. It is a familiar enough gesture, but as I stood facing him I was thinking how strange it is. I was thinking also that it was the first time I had ever had it made to me.

'Getting the truth is going to help,' I said apologetically.

'Perhaps. But she's had more than enough of it. So get along.' He jerked his thumb again. The gesture seemed ludicrous.

'Goodbye, Mrs Powell,' I said, turning.

She didn't answer; she was down close to the child, who was playing with a spoon.

'Cheerio,' I said to her brother. 'No hard feelings.'

He smiled. The smile was happy and open, but not to me; over me. I walked past him, past the shed, and down the side of the house. I got into the car and messed my gears as I was turning. I drove straight back to Cardiff, fast.

6

I had nothing to do then but to go on to Ireland. I was relieved by the effort: returning the car, getting on to the plane. But what was there all the time, at the edge of my mind, was a feeling that I was going the wrong way: that every mile from Pontyrhiw was in the wrong direction, if I was looking for the truth. That was the question, I supposed: the problem from the very beginning. My assignment, certainly, was the shooting of Buxton, but take the whole sequence in order – put it back in order – and Buxton was an incident along the road from Pontyrhiw. To call it an incident diminished it; he had, after all, been shot. But he was now recovering, satisfactorily, in the hospital in Cardiff, while Gareth Powell was dead and his wife and child were without him in that tidy back garden at Pontyrhiw, with her brother coming round, looking after her, trying to see her through it. On any real estimate, that was the case, but nothing works like that. The public story, in any available dominant version, was still the shooting of Buxton.

A public version against my private feelings; was that now the problem? I don't know about private feelings: all I could touch was the rawness, and of course the resentment, of being turned out, seen off, from that private garden. We all say, as reporters, that we are used to brush-offs, but this is differential, like everything else. We are used to brush-offs from all the important people, on those occasional occasions when they don't need us. We are on the other hand used to some welcome, indeed often to respect, from nearly everyone else: the public, vox pop, men in the street, as they're known in the trade. The unexpected exclusion, and even more the immediate rejection, had then cut in hard. It still felt very hard because from the moment I saw Pontyrhiw I was aware of some change: some change in myself. Even before May Powell – the raw face and loose hair – the very bareness of the place, its harsh physical explicitness, had undercut the names and the story and the assigned significance. My relation to it was altering, but then altering in my head: more than in the head, in the nerves and stomach. But that made no difference. I wasn't allocated the privilege of private adjustment. The objective relations were immediately and sharply administered to me; by others, even while my feelings were changing or had changed. Perhaps that's always how it is. People who make a good deal out of private feelings depend, whether they know it or not, on some privilege of distance, within which there is room for their private adjustments to happen. To most of us, close in the world, no time is given for that. The immediate relations are declared, the substantial changes happen, because there are other people there facing you. You may try to feel differently, but that is for later: looking out of the plane at the glitter of the sea; flying away from where the decisive events have occurred.

I was tired that night. I slept early. In the morning, glad of the business, I went to the Tourist Office. I got a list of all caravan hirers and settled down in my hotel room at the phone. It was a long list, but I had names and dates. I was moderately lucky: on the fourth call a booking at Ennis, in

113

County Clare, in the name of Brant, for 3 July. My story was that I was trying to trace friends. I would be unlucky, I was told. The Brant party had returned the caravan on 11 July, then had gone to Shannon to fly back to England. Yes, three in the party: a young man and two young ladies.

I thought about it. I had a long look at a map. Then I rented a car and drove to Ennis. I found the caravan hirer, a friendly man. I told him the same story; I think he didn't believe me, but he was willing to look at the photographs. Yes, surely, that was the party: very pleasant well-spoken young people they were too. Was there anything wrong? No, nothing at all, I was just wanting to contact my friends; what's life without friends? No, he didn't know what route they had gone touring. There are official stops, but they can decide their own. And they were back now in England, for sure; they had all been there, to bring the caravan back, before getting the bus in to Shannon.

I drove round the corner and looked at it all again. All right, it fitted the story: Bill and Rosa and Lucy had been caravanning. But all this really proved was that they'd been in Ennis on the third and eleventh of July. Between these dates, and this was the vital period, with Buxton's shooting on the ninth, they could have been anywhere. A bus ride into Shannon and two of them, at least, could have been back in Britain in an hour or two, then return the same way. But that didn't really seem likely; there was the chance of passports being looked at, as still occasionally happened; booking on the plane would risk being identified later. I got out the map again and I checked on the boats, from Dun Laoghaire, Rosslare, Waterford, Limerick. The service from Limerick particularly interested me; it went to Swansea, a short drive from St Fagans. And on the boats, I knew, there

114

was less chance of being checked.

I was wrong about Limerick, or I think I was. I spent a morning there checking; nobody remembered anyone like any of the three photographs. I tried Waterford next, again with no luck. Rosslare–Fishguard, and a few hours' drive across Wales: that too seemed likely, but again I got nothing. I would try Dun Laoghaire and then fly back. For though I was convinced, privately, not only that it could have been done but that it had been done, yet at the same time I now thought that it would never be proved.

I was driving up to Dublin when I passed a caravan site. I went in and produced my photographs: again trying to trace friends. I was very kindly received; indeed the kindness was embarrassing. And yes, surely this party had stayed there; they remembered them well. What nights would that be? There was checking and consultation. Two nights they'd stayed, they'd liked the place so much. The nights of the eighth and ninth of July.

So that really finished it. Bill and Rosa and Lucy had been in a caravan on Kilmichael Point while Buxton was being shot across the sea in St Fagans. I was dejected, naturally: so much trouble for nothing, yet another false trail. But it was more than that, as it settled. I was also feeling ashamed. I had concocted this theory, about three innocent people. Where did that leave *me*?

I was driving on up the coast, to return the car and go home empty handed, when, again replaying the scene, I saw another possibility. It was Lucy, of course, who had been most directly recognised; this had also been true at Ennis, and it didn't surprise me, having seen her. Lucy had been remembered and with her another girl and a young man. Certainly those two photographs had also been recognised, or so the man had said. But that was a secondary recognition: two other people – a young man and a girl – with Lucy, who was the only one strongly remembered. I think I shouted with delight: not least, perhaps, because it would mean that Lucy was relatively safe. But the others? I drove back and tried again.

It was again disappointing, at first. I put the problem to the site-owner. Other friends had been joining them; there had been a larger party, in different caravans; so was he sure these two had been there? Well yes, as he'd told me the last time. Hadn't it been the young man who had come in to pay? It was him without doubt. 'And the other girl, the smaller, dark-haired one?' Well yes, he'd seen her, around the site, though not to speak to, like the others. 'And it was certainly this girl?' The man called his wife. They both treated me kindly and seriously: this was an important personal problem, people had to find their friends.

Then the woman looked at the photograph again. I could see her doubt growing. I waited, saying nothing.

'Well I couldn't say that it was, and I couldn't say that it wasn't. It's like her, in a way, but not exactly like, if you know what I mean. Still of course it would be her, if she was with the others.'

I didn't like pressing her, but I knew I had to. She stared again at the photograph. It was clear she could get no further. Then I said, remembering: 'The hair, my friend's hair, it's very shining black, raven black.'

I could see at once that I had gained my point.

'Not at all,' the woman said, 'not a shining black. More a brown, a dark brown.'

'No, it's shining black if it's Rosa, that's my friend.'

'Not this one,' the woman said.

116

'It could be a different girl then?' I said, with too much excitement.

She wouldn't be drawn further; she was sure about the hair but more than that she couldn't say. And I could feel the situation tilting; the kindness would soon break. I thanked them, took my photographs and left.

I flew straight back to London. I now had what I wanted, more than I wanted.

7

It was coming Sunday. I had had my three days. But I decided to wait until they called me in. I sat at my desk. I made a list of people and a list of places and dates. A possible sequence began to emerge.

Five people, or more, had planned the shooting of Buxton. I thought I had three of them: Bill and Rosa and Lucy. But then there must also be the fair young man who had rented the car in the name of Tiller, and the brown-haired young woman who, if I was right, had taken Rosa's place in Ireland during the three decisive days. That left open the question of the actual assailant. It could not be either Bill or Lucy: they had been in Ireland. By the same token it could not be the unknown brown-haired girl. And it could not either, I decided, be the young man who had rented the car: the girl in the office had remembered him as tall. Thus, of the five people I had listed, only Rosa could not be ruled out. This was difficult to believe, but not impossible. Given the fact of disguise, which had been clear from the beginning, there was really nothing in the St Fagans description to exclude this ultimate misdirection. At the same time, of course, there was nothing positive to go on: there could be a sixth person, a seventh, and so on. And there was also Mark Evans: my mind kept returning to him.

I went through the list of places and dates.

29 June: the unknown young man rents the car in Tiller's

118

name, London.

3 July: Bill, Lucy and Rosa collect their caravan at Ennis.

8, 10 July: Bill, Lucy and the third girl are in the caravan at Kilmichael Point.

9 July: Buxton shot; Mark Evans returns to London.

10 July: Evans leaves for Zambia.

11 July: Bill, Lucy and Rosa return their caravan and fly back to London.

A lot depended on the hypothesis of the third girl, but if indeed, as I was assuming, Rosa was not with Bill and Lucy at Kilmichael Point, other dates and movements could be inserted:

By 7 July: third girl goes to Ireland (or lives in Ireland).

By 8 July: the 'Tiller' car is left at Fishguard.

8/9 July: Rosa travels Rosslare–Fishguard, collects the car, drives to the St Fagans area.

9 July: Buxton shot; car left in Llandaff.

9/10 July: Rosa returns to Ireland, by a different route (Holyhead–Dun Laoghaire?); rejoins Bill and Lucy at Kilmichael Point; third girl has left.

11 July: caravan returned by Bill and Rosa and Lucy.

This could certainly have happened, and, if so, the intricacy of the operation to cover Rosa, during the three crucial days, pointed overwhelmingly towards her direct involvement in

119

the shooting. Nothing else would have justified so elaborate a misdirection, yet as a misdirection it had the same style as the others in the affair: the Volunteer note; the second cape; the Tiller red herring; the disguise of the assailant. It was still hard to believe, but the whole affair had been planned like that; to leave obvious clues which would come to nothing, and beyond them a series of improbable and untraceable connections. The planning, that is to say, had a common psychology. Moreover, an eccentric psychology. That might even in the end be its weakness.

I sat wondering what to do. My time was up. If I was to get more I would have, at least, to show something of my hand, and the dangers of that were too obvious. If it had been done as I imagined it would be extraordinarily difficult to prove. Probably the only people who ever could prove it, through its complications and persistent false trails, were the police. I would then, in practice, with the bits I had, be not a reporter but an informer. I didn't want that. But I didn't, either, want to let it just fade away. I decided to go in to the office, to risk another assignment, but to use my own time following the real trail. It was a coward's decision, I thought, but then I had coward's luck. When I got to the Insatel office there was nothing urgent waiting for me, and when, later in the day, I ran into Friedmann – he was in a rush as usual; he had taken personal charge of an oil-rig story – I found, to my well-concealed surprise, that he assumed I was working on the Evans telebiography. Not that he promised anything, but he looked forward to seeing a treatment. Would there be anything on paper by the time he got back? Surely, surely. I could have done it on the spot. So I still had my time to myself.

I would have given a good deal to find my two unknowns:

the young man who had rented the car and the other girl in Ireland. But that was the wide world, and meanwhile, at the middle, was Rosa. I began, carefully, tracking her back.

She had graduated in 1984, from the University of London (Sarah had graduated from Cambridge in 1982). Both girls had attended a 'public' (private) day school in Middlesex. Rosa, I found, had been an athlete; she had competed, from school, as a hurdler, in the Inter-County Championships, and again in her first year at university. Not later, apparently, but it seemed to be this experience that had directed her towards the media. In 1983, at university, she had been first Sports Editor and then News Editor of the closed-circuit student television service. Presumably because of this experience she had become, after graduating, a television production trainee with the new Fifth Channel.

That made it easy for me; I had contacts from then on. After her training year she had been given a staff job in direction. She had been very highly rated, but she was not generally liked. One man who had trained with her, and who had not at first got a staff job, said she was superficially clever, very good at planning and routine logistics (in television, often, that means good with hotels and drinks), but owed her advancement, basically, to John Scott-Withers, a wet old man who'd come out of educational radio and was big in the Fifth Channel.

Big with her? No, she'd have killed him. But he'd said, to someone, that she was the new Woman; his mind was back somewhere with *Ann Veronica*. Firm, confident, unassertive, classless: those had been the supporting adjectives. So Rosa had got her two-year staff contract; she had become Rosa, incidentally, for professional purposes, during her second year at university; her friends there still knew her as Rosie, but at the Fifth Channel she was Rosa to everyone.

Politics? Apparently not. An inactive member (sleeping member?) of the Fabian Society as a student. Inactive in the union after she had got her contract. Then at the end of her contract time, with John Scott-Withers scaling new heights of admiration – the new new New Woman – she had been abruptly fired. Officially, of course, it was just that her contract had not been renewed. But my informant was certain: it had been a real firing, following a five-star row, but from so high up that it had taken most people by surprise. He ought to know; he had subsequently got her job. But he'd never seen anything definite. The rumour indicated a Home Study programme which she'd made and which got pulled out on the very last day. But the file had disappeared, and everyone had got the sign to look the other way.

He hadn't looked either way. That said something about him. I got it in an hour and almost started believing in fairies. What she had made, and what hadn't been shown, was a programme in a Social Science course, on Unofficial International Agencies. The stuff that had caused the trouble was about our old friends Political Research and Consultancy: PRC!

Fired August 1986. The trail ended soon after that. A few weeks with Media Research Collective, one of the endless (and necessary) mushroom freelance organisations: free homes for fired media people, retaining their skills and their sense of purpose, not retaining any of the resources they had hitherto ridden on. MRC was no better and no worse than any of the others; the basic fact is that there are just too many of them; or to put it another way, far too many people have been fired. Rosa cleared out, after some internal row.

Since then, nothing registered. MRC had joined up with Community Video. Apparently she hadn't wanted that.

It was all good information, but what was coming through, I realised, was in most ways the wrong personality. This, as I read it, was indeed Sarah Brant's (Sarah Evans's) sister. Except for the PRC incident, this was a career. And God knows John Scott-Withers might have got her into the PRC trouble. If he was back with *Ann Veronica* he might also be back with Open Diplomacy and the Union for Democratic Control and the old pre-war Liberal Establishment. He could have thought you should educate the public by making open fact-finding programmes – *Open Access* was the title of one of his series – about organisations like PRC! But trade unions or business swindles, yes; the hard stuff, no. And then before she knew where she was, her feet wouldn't have touched the ground until her bottom hit the pavement. John Scott-Withers's slippered old feet could never shuffle fast enough to save her. She would be a shocked, surprised, hardworking little girl: good at the logistics, bad at the politics. As of August 1986.

Did that then make sense of what I suspected she had done in July 1987? You never can tell. The whole point about living in a society like this is that people get so confused, by what our theoreticians call the immanent structural contradictions, that they don't have to change, dramatically, in old soul-saving or soul-selling ways. Radically divergent potentials continue to inhabit them. Their ordinary active condition is profoundly divided. Often they don't change at all but simply live with the other half, as the limits and pressures allow. All the way from John Scott-Withers to the shotgun at St Fagans? I would have to try to see.

8

I called the Highgate number and asked for Rosa.

'Speaking.'

Ms Glacier. I warmed to my theme. She knew, perhaps, that I was doing a programme on Mark Evans. I'd had a useful preliminary discussion with Sarah. Now I'd just learned, by chance, of her television experience, and the fact was I would need a couple of weeks' work from someone competent. Was she by any chance interested?

'I've done nothing for nearly a year.'

The glacier was moving. A small trickle of ice-green water. I remembered the John Scott-Withers description, but this was no classless voice: it was just Sarah blunted a bit.

'So I heard, but if you were interested? To talk about it anyway?'

She checked my name again. Then we arranged to meet, next morning, in a pub in Shepherd's Bush.

I had another job before I met her. I needed to know more about Bill Chaney: as himself and as the man who had somehow brought together these improbable co-residents, Rosa and Lucy. Perhaps it was just the usual thing, but I needed to check.

It took a fair time but what I got was straight enough. An Oxford philosopher, early-eighties style, out of work. Meaning he had tried to do some philosophy and found it was out of style. Or, putting it another way, he was not, at that level, particularly good: he had an incurable weakness for general ideas about the world.

I've tracked these careers back so often. The genius child, from what our educated friends call a lower-middle-class family: they can't quite bear to say working-class, once the boy can read and write, but that's what it was: only son, among three daughters, of a Wolverhampton mechanic. Genius at home; brilliant at school (high-flyer, no higher); reasonably clever as an undergraduate; possible as a research student. Then quite impossible, with the aforesaid incurable weakness.

'These bloody little boys,' I remember a man saying, 'coming out of the back streets thinking they'll build systems: all the grime and pretension of the nineteenth century still polluting their brain cells.' Yeah.

The commenced dissertation, on Simmel's distinction between *Einzigheit* and *Einzelheit*. Matter for an editorial in itself, public money being spent on a project like that. Eighteen months and then a growing distance between Simmel and the world. Nine books full of notes, twenty-three draft pages revised to illegibility. Quarrel with his tutor, who said his use of 'disinterested' was a vulgar error: 'It means impartial, not bored.' 'To be impartial is to be bored,' he'd replied. They still come like that sometimes. And he'd set about proving and disproving his point. He'd admitted his boredom, to the point of being positively disinterested in or on Simmel (and it was too late to do anything else). From that admitted boredom he became partisan: he went angrily through no less than four groups in twelve months (that isn't so uncommon: it's how the membership figures keep up). Leafleting, picketing, trying to organise, the usual sectarian bust-ups. Them as he drifted out of the research grant, with

125

the twenty-three pages to show for it – matter for another editorial, adding a point on sheer waste to the note on academic irrelevance – he registered as unemployed (type of work sought: 'philosopher', presumably), and public money was spent again, this time with no editorial. Serve your time and you become a heartbroken victim, condemned to the grey idleness, sad, sad, sad. Three years in London since then: bits of supply teaching; voluntary work with a community association; an advance from a publisher for an introduced translation of Simmel – little progress on that, and the publisher now backtracking, making ominous and relevant remarks about world trade and the price of paper.

Bill Chaney, superfluous man, as they used to say in old Petersburg. I felt I knew him. I could make some relevant comparisons, one rather close to home.

I got to the pub early, for the appointment with Rosa. The bar was full of the usual ego-trips. A combination of making bright deodorant commercials and a modicum of alcohol has this regular liberating effect. I found a corner and watched for Rosa. It was like waiting for a friend.

She came through the doors and looked round. She was in grey jacket and jeans: a sort of battledress. I can just remember when the hard types started wearing this, before it spread through the fringe and finally into the fashion photographs. Like the cord jackets and cravats the bohemian artists imitated from labourers until they became so fancy that serious artists went back into suits. Maybe the parallel doesn't hold; the basic general reason for this style is the washing machine.

I pushed my way through to her and said her name. She didn't smile or make any other adjustment. She was just there, making nothing of anything. I got her a drink: barley wine! We found a table in the corner.

'I was lucky to hear of you,' I said, and tried another smile.

'Lucky?'

'You've not been working, you said?'

'Right.'

'What do you find to do?'

She had lit a cigarette. She looked at me over it and then tapped it, several times, on the brewer's ashtray. There was no loose ash on it. The tapping was like a code. I tried again.

'I heard about your programme.'

'Which?'

'Unofficial International Agencies.'

'Who hasn't?'

'Most people. They buried the file.'

'But passed the word. I'm black.' She took a long drink but left the statutory half-inch for politeness.

'I need some help,' I said, 'at this stage of the research.'

'On Evans?'

'Evans? You're his sister-in-law, aren't you?'

'I don't know what in-law means. Since they changed that Act.'

I got the allusion. I was more interested in the drift. 'You don't get on with him?'

She avoided looking at me. She consumed the polite residue of her barley wine. She moved her feet to get up. I talked fast.

'Did you include his Community Politics Trust, when you were doing your programme on agencies?'

It was a very long shot, but it stopped her. She took the weight off her feet.

'No. Why should I?' She was well controlled, too well controlled. It was obvious there was something.

'It has its problems, surely?'

'I don't know about that. It keeps people off the streets.'

She looked across at me. She was really very like her sister but in a harder-worn, harder-used copy. The same raven hair, the same big dark eyes, but the skin much flatter and duller, the lower cheeks almost grey, and the features more edgy, the mouth dry. As we stayed looking at each other someone turned from the bar and watched her intently: another young woman, fair, bony-faced, with fine prominent teeth: watching Rosa as if in close-up: an intent, learning curiosity.

'Do you have any real information?' Rosa asked.

'Not yet. Only pointing that way.'

'Pointing me that way?'

'If you were interested, yes.'

She thought for some moments, then she moved her feet again. 'No,' she said.

'You're not interested?'

'Yes, I'm interested. But I know a rat-job when I see one.'

'You surprise me. I'd heard you were tough.'

The girl at the bar was still watching intently. She had picked up the tension, though she couldn't know what it was. She wanted to watch, carefully, how Rosa dealt with it: though not Rosa particularly, just this other woman, living through some decision, staring at a man across a table.

Rosa got up, with the girl still watching her.

'Is it a political objection?' I asked, looking up.

'No,' she said. 'I don't buy politics.'

'Did the price get too high?'

She stared down at me. The grey seemed to spread from her cheeks. Then she made an effort. 'No, not at all. I was never much interested.'

'Even at Pontyrhiw?'

128

'Where?'

Not a nerve seemed to move. I pushed round the table and stood ready to walk out with her. She accepted the move and walked out just in front of me. The girl at the bar watched us go, still intently. I found myself wondering how that small observed experience would feed in, somewhere, to some quite other time and relationship. Then we were in the street. We walked together, in an easy stroll. Almost, I thought, as if we liked each other's company and were easy with each other, not needing to speak.

'Lewis Redfern,' she said finally.

'Yes. As I said.'

'I was trying to get it. Birmingham, wasn't it, the carworkers' march? But was it obstruction or assault?'

'Assault. I put my hand on a uniformed sleeve.'

'And then found the price too high.' She couldn't resist turning and smiling at me. It wasn't a pleasant smile. 'You got your political record and then you went to Insatel,' she added, contemptuously.

'Something like that. But still with a choice.'

'What choice?'

'I can put it very simply. I've been working on Buxton, on the shooting. I've found quite a lot that the police don't know. At the same time I've got this assignment on Evans. I can now follow either. I don't suppose it will be both.'

'How could it be both?'

'Are you sure you don't know?'

She looked up at me again. Her moment of aggression had brought back some colour. But there was something else that I couldn't be sure of. I wondered if it was an edge of sadness and doubt.

'I know nothing useful about either,' she said, bravely.

'Tiller,' I said. 'Marcus Tiller. Marcus, Volunteer. That whole elaborate double deception.'

'Double?'

'Yes, don't you know? Tiller was PRC.'

'No, I didn't know that.'

'It was PRC got you fired, wasn't it?'

'No, I don't think so. Not directly, that is.'

'But you had been working on them?'

'Among others, yes.'

'Including the Community Politics Trust?'

She relaxed, visibly. Some pressure was off. Something had gone the right way, the wrong way.

'Look, I'm not going to be able to help you. Why don't we leave it like that?'

'Because it won't stay like that. Your friend Lucy paid Tiller's rent. Somebody hired a car in his name. Somebody left it in Llandaff after Buxton was shot. Somebody stood in for you at Kilmichael Point.'

'Where?' she asked, staring at me. But she was grey again now. She looked up and down the street. 'If the offer's still open,' she said, eventually.

Her calculations were obvious, but they were absolutely cold. Almost any young woman, in a crisis like that, would try at least a smile. Rosa, in her battledress, was still grey and apparently indifferent.

'Here's my address and my number,' I said. 'Just ring or come round, when you're ready.'

She took the card. I thought she shivered slightly: some jerky involuntary movement, but it was quickly controlled.

'Right,' she said.

130

I checked in at the office. There was nothing new. I left a treatment on Mark Evans, which I'd knocked up after breakfast, as some evidence of zeal. Friedmann was still out of town.

I also checked with the police. For obvious reasons I didn't, just then, want any development on Buxton; I was much too exposed. But they had nothing and they were saying nothing, officially.

I took my time getting home. When I got out of the elevator a young woman was standing at the door of the apartment; she was pressing the bell. I couldn't recognise her back: she had long fair hair and an expensive-looking green summer suit.

'He's been out,' I said, coming close behind her.

'Mr Redfern,' she said as she turned. It was Sarah Evans. It took me some moments to be sure. I remembered her face and her voice very clearly, but the blonde wig had altered her remarkably. The deep gloss that I remembered seemed suddenly bizarre, since all her other colouring went with her own raven hair. In this version she was even further from Rosa, whose edgy grey face kept coming back to me.

'I'm sorry,' I said, as she saw my hesitation.

She smiled as I opened the door and stood back to let her go in. She didn't mention the wig; she was too busy being polite about the charming apartment. And I was dazed, both by her – the identity shift had shaken me – and by all the implications. My suspicion of Rosa depended on a much smaller difference of hair colour.

She stood elegantly by the window while I looked for drinks. I was wondering why she had come and whether Rosa had talked to her, which might mean trouble. If manner meant anything there would be no trouble, but manner often doesn't mean anything.

'Who is this?' she asked charmingly. She had picked up a studio photograph on my desk.

'It's my wife.'

'She's charming. I hadn't realised you were married.'

'I am and I'm not. We don't now live together. She's gone back to Canada.'

'I'm sorry. But you keep her photograph.'

'Of course.'

'Mark and I keep photographs too. It's strange, I often think, while we're there together, but when he's away...'

I avoided looking at her. I was running a sequence in which I picked up Mark's photograph and said, brightly: 'Is this your father?' She couldn't have known but she stepped straight on to this ground.

'It fixes a certain moment, a certain age. The image stands still.'

'Not really,' I said.

She looked back at my desk. She had run her own sequence. I expected it to be accurate. 'I saw Rosie this afternoon,' she said, easily. 'She said she'd met you.'

'Yes, we had a talk. I was able to give her some work.'

'So she said. I'm glad. She's extremely able. She won't disappoint you.'

Briefly, in some movement of the mouth, there was a

resemblance to Rosa. It was getting too close. I passed her the drink, and we sat facing each other.

'And if you don't mind me saying so,' she added, gracefully, 'you're extremely able yourself.'

I tried the usual embarrassed grunt.

'Oh yes, Lewis, I've been asking about you. I hear lots of good things.'

'I must remember to thank my acquaintances. Perhaps revive the Christmas card?'

'Well maybe not that. The good things are all work things. Bit on the hard side.'

'That's what work does to us.'

'Your work,' she said.

She was not being charming now. She still smiled a good deal and kept up the hand movements. Without those palmings and wrist-turns she would probably contract aphasia. But the gloss was now operative: a precise tool.

'Lewis, I've talked to Mark on the phone. He's coming straight back.'

'No working party in Mauritius?'

'He's decided to miss it.'

'Then we might, perhaps, bring our meeting forward.'

'He wants to do that. He wants to deal with this himself.'

'Deal with what? The programme?'

'What else?' she said, and again used the charming smile.

'You put it as if there might be something else.'

'Well it had crossed my mind. I mean in the course of getting to know about your work.'

I got up. I needed to move. 'I'm what they call a consultant analyst. That means making maps: political maps. And Mark Evans is a feature: an important feature.'

'Yes, Lewis, I thought you'd say that. But what you

analyse – in fact report – isn't just politics, even radical politics. It's the political underground. Hidden politics.'

'You can't make that clear a distinction. Most of the underground is above ground, shouting, drawing attention to itself. Simply the unofficial opposition.'

'But some are not, and that's why you're employed. To uncover what is hidden.'

'Yes, that sometimes happens, but it's not why I'm employed. Most stories I report are well above the surface. And I'm a reporter, not an informer.'

She smiled. The dark eyes, the creamy skin, were in a different dimension from the shining fairness of the hair.

'What I really ask myself, Lewis – and I suppose ask you – is whether that's a distinction without a difference. I mean, when something is hidden, and you tell the public about it, you're actually telling the police and the law officers.'

'Certainly. If I tell it.'

'You mean you don't always?'

'Certainly not always. For legal reasons, or for my own reasons.'

'And what would your own reasons be?'

'That what was hidden was political and that I was not opposed to it.'

'Giving you the right of judgement?'

'I can't give it to anyone else.'

'Not even to your employers?'

I crossed and sat down again. I looked at her carefully. 'Well Insatel isn't, say, PRC.'

'PRC?'

She did it very nicely: the slight surprise, the smooth distancing, the adjusted indifference. As if her husband had mentioned the name of her lover.

'I just take the example at random,' I said. 'You must have read of the hunt for Marcus Tiller, who was supposed to have shot Buxton. Now he was real underground: an agent paid to get into the radical movement.'

She smiled, again charmingly. 'That's very interesting. But I notice you haven't reported it. Was that for your own reasons?'

'The decision was taken above my head. The organisation Tiller works for has a lot of influence.'

'The one you call PRC.'

'The one they call PRC.'

She smiled and got up. She was preparing to leave. 'Mark will be back late tomorrow. He'll probably ring you himself.'

'Such cooperation!'

'Well why shouldn't he cooperate? If the programme is what you say?'

'What else?' I said and smiled.

She walked past me, on her way to the door. 'Look, Lewis,' she said, turning, 'I happen to know you were assigned to work on Buxton. I've also been told that you don't give up easily. So it crossed my mind, thinking of one or two things you said, that you might still be working on it, and that your idea of a programme on Mark...'

'Well?'

'Well, I wouldn't want you to make that kind of mistake.'

'How could it be a mistake? There's no possible connection. Is there?'

'Of course not.'

'No connection, no mistake,' I said, easily.

She had her hand on the door. She smiled. 'It's your reputation, Lewis. It arrives just a little behind you.'

135

10

I decided, thinking it over, that I was one of the few who did not enjoy Sarah Evans. But that was by the way. It isn't difficult, when you've had my kind of practice – public practice – to know when you're dealing with somebody devious. But that hardly matters. The only interesting question is what they're being devious about.

I decided to concentrate on Evans coming back. I would have liked to talk to Bill Chaney, and of course to Lucy again, but I was in this crunch anyway, having to face Evans, and I needed much more than I had. I had still had no reply from my inquiry in the States. I went down to the office and rang my contact: an Insatel colleague, Peter Jacobs, in New York. He was friendly and informative about everything else; he even gave me the weather. Then, when I insisted, he closed me off.

'It looks very promising, Lewis. But it's nothing like ready.'

'I can understand that. But it's getting urgent this end.'

'Which part of it exactly? The Welshman?'

'Sure. That mainly.'

'The problem, Lewis, is the ramifications.'

'Well, of course. Can't we share them?'

'Share a bag of air?'

'Open skies,' I said.

He wouldn't talk any more. That indeed made it

promising. No competent reporter would talk that sort of material through on a transatlantic line. After further persuasion he said he'd put what he had on the plane: the regular Insatel freight bag. But only when we'd registered a lock: that's an internal procedure, when more than one reporter is working on a story, especially from different stations, and we register the lock through the network, so that no one can do a quick steal. I waited for the bag. It didn't come on the plane he'd promised. Through some inefficiency my own lock had been delayed, though his had come through and I'd looked at it and been puzzled. The title he'd registered was The Volunteers.

I had never seen that before, in any specific use. It was galling, of course, because it's my business to know all these names, even when they appear and disappear as often as pop groups. I mean take every permutation you can devise, of radical, socialist, communist and revolutionary, of league, group, front, party, centre and so on, national and international: it's still the differences that matter, to them and to me. The Volunteers, on its own, was quite new, and of course I didn't need prompting to remember the Tiller note. And was this what I had got in reply to an inquiry about Mark Evans and the Community Politics Trust? I was actually waiting in the Despatch Office when the next bag came in. An envelope from Jacobs was in it. A thin envelope.

It was a guarded sheet. He was adding his private lock. But the material I'd been looking for was there, almost incidentally, since he was clearly not much interested in it but in something else it led into. For me, however, it was crucial. The Community Politics Trust had been principally financed, through intermediate foundations, by PRC, on its Special Service budget. And his information was that Evans had discovered this, on a trip to Washington about eighteen months back. He'd evidently not known it when the Trust was founded and he was made its Director. Then apparently, when he'd found out, he'd ranted: that was Jacobs's word. Ranted for several days: threatened publicity and exposure. None had come, so end of story. Presumably he enjoyed the money and wanted to go on getting it.

I thought about it, just glancing over the rest, which was where the lock had been put on. Was this then the truth of Mark Evans, that he had got to know that he was directing a tainted organisation and had decided to keep quiet about it? I could imagine that: out of evil good shall come, and other conventional maxims. But still Evans, as such, was not the problem. Nor was his Trust, though I would file that away. I could see, quite easily, what PRC would be getting for its money: the lists of names, primarily; people the Trust funded and even more, whenever they needed it, a fairly direct channel to slip somebody in. Evans himself? I didn't think so, though the possibility was obvious. People came to him all the time, described all their schemes, and though most of them were soft stuff there would be some others. You can't have a strategy of general infiltration without a few bizarre cases: unarmed combat training in the adolescent adventure playground – that had once actually happened, but it had been stopped within a week; people just came and watched and wrote letters to the papers. No, the real thing to watch, in the PRC book, would be the straight funding: groups doing what they said but making time for a bit of the other.

I didn't believe that such simple double-dealing was in Evans's character. Not from what I knew of him, but I would have to wait and see. What was much more interesting was

138

the possible bearing on Buxton, but at first I didn't see this. I had jumped at the stuff about the Trust and PRC, and the rest, as I said, was very guardedly put down. It might be coincidence; it probably was, Jacobs carefully explained. But he'd tracked back on the leak to Evans: the leak that PRC was financing him. It had come, he believed, not only from inside but from very high up: too high to be a case of the counter-penetration we both knew about. Indeed it was not directly from PRC at all but from their effective customers for the Special Service: a group known simply as the Board. Someone as exalted as that – evidently Jacobs knew his name but he wasn't telling – had made contact with Evans and had told him the truth. But why was then the question. Not out of pity or spite for Evans, but perhaps as part of some other proposition. That was where Jacobs started digging.

He hadn't put the dirt in the bag. All he said was that he thought there was something going, something I might care to look out for. He wasn't even sure of the name, perhaps it was just a general reference, but a young woman in Washington, in circumstances he didn't elaborate on and I was grateful for that – I've given up reading that stuff – had mentioned the Volunteers and not long after had been as worried as hell, trying to pull it back, steer him off, have him sample anything else in the world. Incidentally, he added, she knows your Evans.

It wasn't making sense. If it was anything of the kind that Jacobs suspected, about the last thing they would have anything to do with would be St Fagans and that note signed Marcus, Volunteer. The coincidences, nevertheless, were beginning to mount, and some of them, inevitably, would be genuine connections. In any event my immediate problem was solved. I had material to put to Mark Evans. 'What else?' as Sarah would have said, with that charming smile that I now fully saw the need for. They were sitting, after all, on a pretty massive fault, and the last thing they'd want was the cheerful arrival of a persistent young man with a drill.

11

Meanwhile there was Rosa. I was waiting to hear from her, wondering what she would bring. But as the hours passed I began wondering if she would get in touch again at all. If my calculations about her were right I had, after all, quite effectively alerted her. She might simply decide to skip. She would know that the only evidence I really had against her was inference: nothing hard, that I could simply betray. And it was then a matter of character: would she just put herself out of reach, knowing that the crucial facts were well covered; or would she brazen it out, or at least stay close to me, to be sure what I was doing? She was taking her time to think it over: putting it to Chaney, perhaps, as a philosophical problem: a definition of *Einzigheit*.

I had about decided that they would be deep in that for the night when the phone rang.

'Rosa Brant.' The same cool, unwavering, putting down, voice.

'I was waiting to hear from you.' Two could play that game.

'I had several things to look through. But I now have some material.'

'Good. Can you bring it here in the morning?'

'No. Not your flat.'

'Well the office then?'

'No thank you.'

'Then shall I come round and see you?'

'No. I can give it to you tonight. Do you know the Finsbury Park gates, by the station?'

'I can find it.'

'In about half an hour?'

'Three quarters it would take me. But why there?'

'Think it over. Are you coming?'

'Yes,' I said, and hung up.

I set off straightaway. It was past ten o'clock and already dark. As I sat in the train, mostly with people going home, I went over the possibilities. At this time of night it wouldn't exactly be the safest spot in London, and Rosa, if I was right, was in a group that had staged an attack. But even as I thought that I more or less discounted it: if I understood this group, it wouldn't at all be their style. The more probable reason, I guessed, was to avoid talking indoors, where a recording would be easier. But this was amateurish, if so. If I had wanted to record her I could have done it from my pocket. I'd actually opened a drawer and picked up the little recorder, before I set out, but then decided against it. My reason, really, was that I trusted it more in my head, where I could decide whether or not to use it. Still, she was arranging a deliberate secrecy: the park, this late. It isn't every young woman of Rosa's age who would stand there this late, waiting. But then perhaps not alone. Perhaps flanked by the philosopher-king, the philosopher-militant. Or perhaps by the young man who had rented Tiller's car. Anyway, on my side, a sudden arrangement: take it or leave it: no time to make any real plans.

I walked out of the station, which felt very empty. In the street the pubs had closed, but there were still a few people around. I walked along and looked across at the park gates.

142

I kept on walking. The street wasn't well lighted, and across the road I probably wouldn't be recognised. There was nobody there; at least I saw nobody. The expanse of the park was very dark beyond.

I crossed over further up, and came quietly back. When I was level with the gates I still saw no one, and I decided to keep on walking. I was almost past when the voice came.

'Here.'

It was unmistakable, that cool voice. I was made to feel foolish, as if I had got myself lost.

I turned and looked for her. She was standing in the shadow of one of the gate pillars. She didn't move, so I went across to her.

'I'm glad you saw me passing.'

'Twice,' she said.

I looked around. There was nobody near us. I paid special attention to the shadows, but so far as I could see there was nothing.

'It's too late for a drink,' I observed.

'Shall we walk?' she said. It wasn't really a question.

She turned into the park, and I walked beside her. We went out across the grass. There were more shadows now, including the shadows of what are still officially called courting couples, though when you couldn't avoid looking there wasn't much you'd call courting going on. Rosa and I, presumably, would be taken for the same, and that, at least, was a laugh.

'You said you have some material?'

'Yes.'

'On what?'

'On what you asked for.'

'Mark Evans?'

143

'Yes, in effect.'

'Will his wife approve?'

'Never mind that.'

'She's your sister, Rosa. Soon after I'd talked to you she came to see me, when she could as easily have phoned. She even took the trouble to put on a wig.'

'What does her appearance matter?'

'It would be a nice defence line for Kilmichael Point. Don't tell me you haven't seen that.'

She didn't answer immediately. We were walking deeper into the wide empty area of grass. I kept my eyes well open. They had adjusted now to the dim light.

'I don't know what you're talking about,' the cool voice came. 'But I'd better make it clear that I'm not discussing any of that.'

'Very prudently,' I said.

'No. It's just I can't be bothered chasing all your fantasies. You'd have to find a different person for that.'

I listened, but let it drip off. With Rosa, evidently, offence was a habit, a cooled, tempered habit.

'All right, be yourself then,' I said.

'You evidently know about PRC,' she began.

'Of course.'

'Including the Special Service?'

'Yes.'

'You were right, incidentally. Tiller was in it. He was on a particular assignment. I'll come to that.'

'It connects?'

'It may. But it isn't important. What is important, and what you don't know, is that among various covers that PRC has financed is the Community Politics Trust.'

'No,' I said. 'I didn't know that.' It secured her triumph

and would bond her assurance.

'Well, it's so. I can prove it if necessary.'

'It's very surprising. Surely Mark Evans doesn't know?'

'Yes, he knows. He has known for more than a year.'

'And kept quiet about it?'

'Of course. Wouldn't you?'

'You say he has known for more than a year. How long have you known?'

'For longer than that.'

'While you were working on that programme?'

'Yes. That's when I got it. That's also why I was got rid of.'

'Are you sure? It seems so unlikely.'

'I can tell you the exact sequence. I took this to Evans. I didn't know he already knew. But it was soon obvious that he did and that he intended to stop me. He tried one way and failed. He tried the other and succeeded.'

'Which way failed?'

'Let's keep to the main point. He went to the Controller. He knows all the ropes and he still has several contacts, from when he was a Minister. He got the programme stopped, on the very last day.'

'And got you fired?'

'Not directly, no. That was their decision.'

'It must have been very difficult for you,' I said. 'I mean since your sister is married to him.'

'Yes,' she said, playing it straight back.

'It would still be bad for her. I mean now you're giving it to me.'

'I haven't finished. When you hear the rest you may forget Mark Evans. Or at least be less interested in him. In that side of it anyway.'

145

I could see a park bench ahead. I steered her towards it and suggested we should sit down. She agreed, indifferently. Yet in some way it relaxed her. When she spoke again her voice was quite different: younger, more neutral.

'What do you know about the Volunteers?' she asked, looking at me.

'Which volunteers?'

'That means you don't know. The advantage of the name is that it sounds so general. In fact it's very specific.'

'A radical group?'

'You could say that.'

'In this country?'

'In several.'

'Then I certainly should have heard of them. But I haven't.'

'You see,' she said, and her original tone had returned, though with less conscious offence.

I was still looking around. The path we were sitting by was empty, but I thought I could hear footsteps along it, some way up.

'Is it intended to be secret?' I asked.

'Of course.'

'You're not in it by any chance?'

'Me? No. Absolutely no.'

'That sounds as if you'd considered it.'

'Yes. Well I was asked.'

'By whom?'

'By Evans.'

The sound of footsteps had stopped. I looked beyond her in the direction from which I had heard them, but I could see nothing. I needed to look, but also, of course, I needed time to think.

'Mark Evans is in this group?'

'No, not exactly. He's what they call a sponsor.'

'A nice respectable thing to be. A nice safe thing to be.'

'No, you don't understand. The whole thing is safe.'

'But radical?'

'They think so.'

'Go on,' I said.

'Well you'll hardly believe it. It's a variant, really, of the old Fabian permeation. Of course everyone says that and they don't deny it. They just say it's different because the State is now different.'

'The State?'

'Exactly. Of course most of the groups do permeation of a kind: permeation, infiltration, entrism. But most of it, I don't need to tell you, is into related or possible organisations: other parties, the unions, tenants' associations and so on.'

'And into each other,' I said. 'Interlocking membership. Where would we be without it?'

'Exactly. Or then the other line. The Communist Party for example. Party members are encouraged to work hard and gain influence in their own relevant spheres, but always, of course, to identify themselves as Communists, to add to the prestige of the party and to have influence, that way, on merit.'

I could hear the footsteps again, but they seemed to be moving away. I realised, as I heard them, that I had relaxed with Rosa, relaxed too far, but she hadn't left me much choice: sitting there in the dark discussing variants of tactics – it seemed like half my life.

'The Volunteers,' she continued, 'are in these terms quite different. They assume, on the one hand, that ordinary

147

permeation, of popular organisations – and of course their institution and maintenance – is very well provided for. They believe, on the other hand, that working openly for influence, while declaring your position, is at best very limited. What influence you may get is neutralised by the fact that in a crisis you can be identified and isolated. I think on that they're right.'

'Right and wrong, who knows? When it's all so wrong.'

'The tactics?' she said sharply.

'No, not the tactics. The results. The results are all wrong. Look around you.'

It wasn't the perfect phrase, sitting there in the darkness, but she didn't take me up on it. I simply blamed myself for letting the sadness show through. Not because it makes you vulnerable, but because it makes things worse. I went on staring past her, into the empty darkness.

'The two mistakes then,' she continued calmly. 'Entry only into left or popular organisations; entry anywhere but always identified. It's in learning from those mistakes that they call for volunteers.'

'To do what is the question.'

'To go into the State apparatus: the modern State apparatus. Central government, local government, the army, the police, the law...'

'I know the list,' I said, impatiently.

'Management,' she continued, 'the public and private corporations. And of course the media.'

'But this is fantasy, Rosa. You must know it's fantasy.'

'I may know and you may know, but they don't. This is exactly what they're doing, at least what they've started to do.'

'But don't they realise... ?' I said, yet I was tired of

arguing, and my voice dropped, involuntarily.

'Yes,' she said, 'they know very well that it's difficult. They also know that it will take a long time. But they're ready for that. The whole thing is long term. And it has to be slow for one particular reason, which I'm sure you've seen already.'

I was by now very tired. I hadn't realised how tired. I could have just stretched out on the bench and slept. It wasn't an ordinary tiredness of the body but a deep fatigue, from what felt like inside: a kind of darkness and numbness just flooding through me, so relentlessly that it frightened me, and I tried to jerk myself out of it. And this girl beside me in the darkness – Ms Glacier I fought to remember – was being pleasant, easy, even flattering. I felt a sense of great danger, an overwhelming danger. She was still speaking, in that younger, more neutral voice.

'Every institution of that kind has its own defences,' she was saying. 'One of the main things they look out for – it's become second nature – is exactly this kind of penetration. If you've got a record you're not out, you never get in.'

'It varies,' I struggled to say.

'Of course. There are soft parts. The universities, the schools, the operative parts of the media. But the rest is very hard, at the levels that matter. And it's just those levels the Volunteers want to get to.'

'I want to swim the Atlantic,' I said, yawning.

'Yes,' she said, amused, but she didn't laugh. 'And that's what makes it slow. They have to confine themselves to people without records: not just open records, militancy of any kind, but traceable membership, even traceable interest.'

'Fool's gambit,' I said. 'If they're not even interested what

149

on earth can they volunteer for?'

'I said traceable interest.'

'*You* said?'

'They say. I was trying to present them as they would present themselves.'

'That's generous.'

'No, it isn't. It's reporting.'

I had to stand up. I stamped my feet and swung my arms.

'Are you cold?' she asked, surprised.

'No, not cold. Numb.'

'Would you rather walk?'

'Yes, I'd rather walk.'

We set off across the grass. We didn't speak for some time.

'I had no record,' she said suddenly. 'You should know this, you researched me. No record, no traceable interest.'

'You have now,' I said. 'Once you started to do something.'

'The programme?'

'That too.'

I could feel her tighten up. It would make things easier, but I knew, suddenly, that I didn't want it. I couldn't, at least now, fight her or anyone any more. But also, by verbal habit, I couldn't really stop myself.

'You remember St Fagans?' I said.

'No.' The voice was very cold again.

'I'm not talking about Buxton,' I said. 'I was just remembering the park. Walking like this across the grass, with the folk memories, the folk memorials, all around you.'

'There's nothing here,' she said.

'Oh yes. It's here. It just hasn't been put together.'

'Parks are better as parks, not made into museums.'

'Could you run across this park?' I asked, quietly.

She didn't answer.

'I'm not proposing we should,' I said. 'My mind was just playing with variations. Variations of traceable interest.'

'I don't know what you mean.'

'You were an athlete, Rosie.'

'At school.'

'And university.'

'For a while.'

'What was it, the training? Did it take up too much time?'

'Something like that.'

'And you say these volunteers...'

'They get them,' she said.

'To go into the State apparatus? To work normally, to attend to their careers, to show no traceable interest in anything else?'

'That's right.'

'I bet they get them,' I said, feeling stronger. 'Why shouldn't they get them? All the career boys and girls, set on happy accumulation, but of course they're different, they're special. They're volunteers. To succeed.'

'Yes. That makes it easier. Of course it makes it easier. But still they've made their commitment.'

'Who hasn't?' I said. 'But a commitment to nothing. A commitment that will never be called.'

'They say it will be called.'

'When?'

'When it matters. In a crisis. When they have got thoroughly inside.'

I could feel the tiredness flooding back, but again I overrode it. 'So then many will be called,' I said brightly, 'and two or three will answer. By that time, Rosie, they'll have become their offices, they'll be their own crusts.'

'You're probably right.'

'Only probably? Christ, Rosie, where have you lived? Haven't you watched your friends growing up? Haven't you seen what happens to people?'

'A bit. Yes.'

'Then what's this all about? It's just another fantasy.'

'There's the oath,' she said.

'Oh my God, they don't have an oath?'

'I don't know what it is. I know that they take it. And it's recorded. Taped.'

'Who keeps that?'

'I don't know.'

'A little treasure house that would be. A pot of gold for a blackmailer.'

'Or a reporter,' she said.

We walked on some way without speaking.

'You know the real model for this,' I said. 'It's a well known method in espionage. Two methods really: planting an official and planting a sleeper.'

'Yes, I thought of that.'

'Are you sure it isn't? Just espionage, I mean?'

'In the first instance it isn't.'

'Do they have to pass information, as they get it, or do they simply wait for the one great day?'

'No passing of information, except on something very important and urgent.'

'And who decides that?'

'They do.'

I hesitated. 'And you're sure Mark Evans is in it?'

'Yes. As I said, he asked me to join.'

'To drop your programme, stay on in the Channel and become a Volunteer?'

'Yes.'

'A convenient offer for him to make.'

'Yes. That's what I thought.'

The bad tiredness had gone, but an ordinary tiredness had replaced it. I thought, in any case, that I would get no more.

'Do you feel like running?' I asked.

'Running? Why?'

'I feel like running. It's a way of blowing the tensions.'

'You mean actually running?'

'What else?'

I felt her look across at me. We could see the gates, about two hundred metres away.

'Race you,' I said suddenly, and started.

I ran full out but almost at once she was past me. Over fifty and then a hundred metres I just watched her going away. Past that I kept up, and in the last fifty metres I was even gaining a little, though I didn't catch her. She stopped at the gates and looked round. I could see her face in the light from the street. She was flushed and exhilarated but breathing quite steadily. My own breathing was rough.

'Thanks,' I said.

She smiled and looked pleased. We turned and walked towards the station. I kept the talk to nothing. I didn't mind that she had steered me off Buxton and St Fagans. I had my confirmation that she could run that fast. The attack on Buxton had depended on that.

We got a late train. I offered to see her home and she looked up and said: 'Where's that?' But I didn't press it, and when it came to the point she just got up at her station and clearly didn't expect me to follow her.

'I'll be seeing you,' I called after her.

'Goodnight,' she said.

153

PART THREE

I found myself out in the street. I was walking steadily along the pavement, with people moving around me, and I did not know how I had got there; I had no memory at all of leaving my room and coming down in the lift. As I began to notice my surroundings I felt only a sense of displacement. It was as if I was moving in two ways, two places, at once.

I eventually remembered what I was supposed to be thinking about. It was not Pontyrhiw, which, by Insatel standards, was dead; only Buxton was alive. I recalled a telecast reference: 'The riot at Pontyrhiw, in which, it will be remembered' (because it is not remembered) 'there were casualties, one of them fatal.' But presumably I am employed because I can make connections. Friedmann knows this in theory, and from past cases, but in every new one he forgets it. So I knew what he knew I should be doing.

I went back to the hotel room. I kept an eye on the screens. Already there were identikit pictures of the young man in the cap, with reproductions of the note from 'Marcus, Volunteer'. Most of the pictures were already labelled Marcus, and there was a free range on Volunteers, with not a fact in sight.

My own thoughts still moved in another direction. Of the hundreds of words in that Pontyrhiw pamphlet, only six now stuck, as I got back to my job: 'The television crew were already filming.' I had seen nothing of Pontyrhiw when it happened. I had been in Italy on one of Friedmann's more improbable hunches. And there was no film of the attack itself. As the pamphlet said, the crew had been moved before it began. But what interested me more now was the group outside the gates, the unofficial group. There might well, in passing, be film of them.

I got on to the Insatel library. I dialled a line and got what film there was played through. It looked different from the pamphlet but it didn't contradict it. I froze several frames of the group outside the gates. It was a very long shot, but suddenly I froze in my turn. Standing among the group, not prominently but, as I stopped it, quite visibly, was a bearded young man in a blue denim cap. He was between two girls: one tall and fair, one shorter and very dark. Then someone walked across, and they were gone from sight again.

I stared at the frames for some minutes. Then I started checking to get the names of the crew. One of them, Carl Howard, I had occasionally worked with. It took three calls to get him, but I would have made three hundred. I kept it professional. I was working, I told him, on the Pontyrhiw inquiry; I'd been checking back through the film.

'You know they moved us out, Lewis?'

'Yeah.'

'So it's only atmosphere stuff. If we could have got the army...'

'Yeah.'

'But they were taking no chances. They didn't want it on film.'

'Yeah. Too bad. Still I thought I'd ask. In case you'd seen any more.'

'Not a chance, Lewis. They closed us right down.'

'Yeah. Too bad. And before that, I suppose, the strikers

57

if it were young; the obvious strength of the tall, heavy body, in the brown drill suit and the scarlet jersey shirt; the open confidence and friendliness of the whole expression and movement, coming powerfully and irresistibly towards me.

'Mr Redfern.'

The voice was not only identifying me; it was congratulating me. I took his hand but turned slightly away. He steered me towards the sofa, and we sat at opposite ends of it. A girl came in with coffee and biscuits, and he was attentive in handing things to me. I hesitated over the biscuits: an unfamiliar brand. PRC: the better biscuit. What it actually said was Rich Cream.

'Sal's told me about your ideas,' he said, smoothly.

'Just a notion or two.'

I was looking through a window at the extraordinary canopy of leaves. It was strange to be on that kind of level with trees, staring on equal terms into their upper branches. Yet it's a common upper office experience. It assuages the administrative ego.

He was going on talking, setting his own scene. I realised, suddenly, that all the time he was speaking he was watching me intently. I was embarrassed by this but found the embarrassment ironic; it is usually I who am cast as the watching devil, the staring professional intruder. It was a status problem really. I can deal with these people in the street or in an argument, but whenever I meet them in their own formidable places, I am shamingly nervous of them: not meaning to be but just finding myself awkward, all thumbs and banalities, while they go on communicating their own confident world. What makes it worse is that under the numbness I start an aggressive silent braying about them: so excessively rude that in fact it builds them up in my mind.

It's at the edges like these that we all learn a style.

I could make out, meanwhile, what he was doing. I didn't know how much Sarah, Sal, had told him, but he was making a fast, clean, parliamentary run for his own version of what we had to talk about: as assured and as safe as a civil servant's draft of a ministerial answer. I let him develop it: his natural pleasure at the idea of the programme; his natural reservations about self-advertisement; his natural curiosity about the particular themes I had thought to develop. He kept mentioning the organisation, but even if he hadn't, the three words of its title – community, politics and trust – would still have come through as his self-definition. I began imagining him proposing to Sarah, Sal. He could make even a proposition, let alone a proposal of marriage, sound like a welfare project. But as I went on sitting and listening, still awkward with the coffee cup, I began to get some of the secondary effects: the things people said about him when they came back with grants, or even without them; the basically decent man; the nice man.

I put down the cup, with an effort. I turned and looked at him. His smooth sentence didn't break, but the signs of alarm, perhaps even of fear, were unmistakable. I found this astonishing, though I knew he had cause. Then I remembered the old saw: when you're nervous of somebody just proceed on the assumption that he's equally nervous of you.

He'd completed his run. It was now obviously my turn. I looked into his face, trying the usual decipherment back across the years: the same face young, the face at eighteen, before the adult knockabout started. I may have been wrong, but what I seemed to see was a face that made me hesitate: sharp, clever, aggressive, impatient, no kindness at all, and most of the strength negative. A hard, critical, biting face. It blurred again almost at once: the exceptional geniality, the wise patience of the middle-aged Director came steadily over it. But I made my reservation. This was not a man to take lightly. This was even a man to stay clear of. And was it, or wasn't it, too late for that?

'It's straightforward as you describe it,' I said.

'And as you would describe it?'

'I'm just a reporter. I work to my brief.'

'A consultant analyst, actually. I think that's the phrase Sal reported.'

'It comes to the same thing. At least on a programme like this. I mean in the ordinary sense there would be nothing to report. You haven't done anything.'

'I suppose not.'

'In the terms of news editors, that's all I mean. You haven't stolen anything or shot or raped anybody. You haven't even betrayed a political secret.'

He looked at me sharply. The younger face came back for a moment. 'What a frustrating world these editors must live in,' he said. 'With most of their fellow human beings doing nothing at all.'

'What fellow human beings? That's an extraordinary assumption about editors. That's radical talk.'

He smiled and ran his fingers through his hair.

'Anyway,' I continued, 'there are always more than enough who meet the qualifications.'

'Yes,' he said sadly, 'it's a bloody enough world.'

The sadness sounded genuine. I wondered, briefly, if I could apply for membership. It would be an easier way to live: the long sighing of the just; the mature, sad consciousness of non-intervention.

'And against it,' I said, 'what do we really have? Your kind of effort?'

'I agree. It's inadequate.'

'It drains your blood, and still it's inadequate. That would be one way of telling it.'

'A story of our time?'

'Of a bit of our time. There are other ways, of course.'

'For example?'

'For example the active groups: the opposition. When you came out of Parliament you thought about them.'

'The new constituencies?'

'And the new agencies. You must have known what you were doing when you wrote that new preface.'

'Yes, I thought I knew.' Very guarded now.

'You were telling my generation something. Telling us with authority what we already suspected. That the game was over. The parliamentary game. The representative game.'

'That the game had limits, I thought I was saying.'

'No, you'd said that before, and it wasn't bad news. All that really promotes is the limits of the possible and then the art of the possible: the usual political crap.'

'It had seemed more than that.'

'Not really. Set the limits of representative democracy, there's still a decent shared area beyond them: community politics, voluntary work, single-issue campaigns. In fact where you've got to. Where you're now at, officially.'

'Officially?'

'Well all that we see of you in public, that is.'

He smiled defensively. At the same time he stiffened his back and seemed to be summoning his strength. 'Do you think there is more, Mr Redfern?'

'I know there is more,' I said, looking away.

161

He barely hesitated. His control surprised me. I had got so used to thinking of him as soft that I wasn't prepared for it.

'You think my arguments have had other effects,' he said, neatly. 'You think that in loosening people's confidence in the political system I've opened the box and now anarchy is loose.'

'No, don't overestimate your influence,' I said. 'People lost confidence in the political system from direct experience: that it didn't solve their problems.'

'To articulate a truth is still to take responsibility,' he insisted. 'When I'd shown the limits of representative democracy I could point in only one way: to direct political action.'

'Of every kind?' I asked.

'Not positively, of course. But since the representative system is there to contain action, to defuse it, I can't escape responsibility for what happens when it's weakened, whether I approve of what is done or not.'

'All the way?' I asked.

'In that sense, all the way.'

'All the way to the shooting of Buxton.'

He stood up. 'But I had warned that this would happen,' he said, firmly. 'And it wasn't I, it was Buxton, who crossed that barrier. When he sent in the army, against an ordinary occupation, he loaded the gun that was to shoot him.'

'You'd say this in public?'

'Of course. But then,' sadly, 'there's no hard evidence to show that he actually ordered it.'

I paused and looked up. I needed that moment to clear my mind. I found myself respecting him, but that wasn't the problem. What mattered was that he was defining the questions and answers. He had made me his interviewer, and himself the public figure. All politicians, of course, are skilful at this, but he wasn't in office; he hadn't the usual base. What was most significant was that he had steered our talk to such general questions, when I had particular questions. Very competently, he had made the inquiry an interview.

'I can see that you've been thinking about these general points,' I said. 'Perhaps composing your apologia.'

'Not an apologia. I have no need to defend myself.'

'You're doing it very well. And established opinion would think you had need to: the high-minded man who provokes disorder and violence.'

'That charge would be useful. I could show the roots of the disorder and violence.'

'Yes, quite possibly. But it isn't, surely, quite as simple as that. To sustain your position you've had to live in the world.'

'Of course.'

'Your Trust,' I said. 'Are you happy about that?'

'It's good and necessary work.'

'I agree. But its funding? Does it ever worry you where the funds really come from?'

'It's on the record,' he said. He was still looking down at me. He had clasped his hands behind his back. His shoulders stood out squarely.

'A version is on the record,' I said.

He remained quite still.

'But you have reason to doubt it?' he asked.

'Not so much a *reason* to doubt it. I've got evidence to show that the real source is different.'

'You could produce that evidence?'

'It could be produced.'

He looked around the office. I thought he must be seeing it as pathetically modish: the executive comfort with the community politics trimmings.

'You're bluffing, Mr Redfern,' he said, coolly.

'No,' I said.

'Oh but you are. I even know what you'll say next. You'll revive this story about the Trust being funded by PRC.'

I tried to look steadily back at him, though this had taken my breath away. He was again much stronger, much more active, than I had at all allowed for.

'It's been carefully planted,' he said, 'in an attempt to hurt us. When I first came across it, in Washington as it happened, I wanted to expose it as the lie it is. I informed the Trustees. I asked for their authority to bring it into the open, to have an independent inquiry and a published report. I didn't get that authority. The Trustees felt, a majority felt, that the publicity would harm us, even if, as was certain, the charge was entirely disproved. I thought of resigning. It seemed the only course. But I was urged to stay on, and in the end I agreed, on one simple condition: a rigorous private inquiry, by persons agreed between the Trustees and myself. That inquiry took place. I have its report. And it shows, conclusively, not only that the story is a lie – that PRC has never funded us, directly or indirectly – but that the source of the lie is PRC itself. It's a not unfamiliar tactic, in so devious an organisation. They can use their own notoriety, the near certainty that most people will believe anything bad about them, as a way of harming others and of confusing people. Using your own mud to smear your opponents: that's sharp, wouldn't you say?'

'It would be sharp if it were true. Can I see that report?'

'No, you can't. It's a private report, as I've already

explained. And that isn't my fault. I wanted it public.'

I nodded as if perplexed or sympathetically baffled. He didn't respond. He just stood where he was and watched me.

'There's only one situation in which you would see it, Mr Redfern. If it happened that you published this story, perhaps as an item in what you had represented as a general programme about me, you would certainly see this report. You would see it in court.'

'Is that a promise?' I said, smiling.

'Sal was right,' he said. 'Your reputation does seem to arrive just a little behind you.'

'She probably got that from her sister. From Rosa.'

I didn't expect a reaction. I was just trying to push some of the disadvantage back. But the effect was immediate. The hands came from his back. The shoulders were loosened and lowered. I didn't understand it, at the time. So I made a mistake.

'Rosa, after all, believes this story too. In fact she came to you with it, when she was doing her programme. She says you stopped the programme and got her fired.'

'No, that's a fantasy. I told her what I've told you.'

'Which still stopped her story being published, however.'

'Stopped a lie being published.'

'Can I then check with your Trustees?' I asked, making another mistake.

'Yes,' he said at once. 'I'll tell them to expect you.'

And you couldn't get fairer than that, along any line I was professing.

It was only when I was being shown out, after a few softer words and an agreement that we would both think it over and then, in a while, get in touch again, that I realised how effective his control had been. For what, in the end, did I

165

care about the Trust and PRC? I wouldn't have published it anyway. There was no point in knocking the Community Politics Trust: soft option as it is. And there's no news in exploding a rumour that's been virtually a secret. So the whole thing was a sidetrack from my real investigation. And it was a sidetrack that others had managed. 'In so devious an investigation,' I found myself saying, adapting Mark Evans's phrase. And the deviousness, I now saw, wasn't only a response to that complicated misdirection which had throughout accompanied the attack on Buxton. It went much deeper: it was a confusion, that came through as deviousness, in myself.

7

Friedmann was back, and he wanted to see me. It was the day after my failure with Mark Evans, and when I went in I even felt glad, for once, that Friedmann existed. He would probably have news of some tremendous political development: *Capital* would be on sale in a High Street bookshop in Blackburn; a student who'd once read Lenin would have been seen talking to a trade unionist; dummy grenade ashtrays were being made on the shopfloor of a motor components factory. Something like that, and anything like that would be welcome. It would let me out, into a defined world.

Friedmann, even behind his huge desk, looked like intellectuals should look but in my experience never manage to: thoughtful, mature, concerned. It's an easy enough make-up; it even happens naturally: the high forehead (receding hair), the glasses (fading eyes), the look of a wild hawk (money problems).

'Come in, come in, Lewis.' He makes even polite indications sound urgent.

'You've seen this, I suppose?'

I took the paper he handed me. The shotgun at St Fagans had been traced to a theft, more than a year ago, in Tiverton, but there was nothing between the robbed farmer and the Cilewent Farmhouse: just the ordinary greyness of a common crime.

'It confirms your feelings, I expect.'

I did a quick check on what feelings I ought to have; I didn't want to break his concentration. 'Yes,' I said.

'You did very well, Lewis. You got further than anyone.'

'No, I felt I didn't get anywhere. It kept slipping me.'

'Tiller and PRC was a good enough break.'

'Yeah.'

Who the hell had briefed him on that?

'And that, I suppose, was the big one? Your three days, you remember?'

'Sure. But it didn't come out.'

'I know. And it's as well. We could never have proved it. And now we don't need to.'

'Because the Buxton affair is dead?'

'Well it is, Lewis. A minor Minister gets a few pellets in his calves. Christ, when you think of the world!'

He had lent me his aeroplane to trace those few pellets. But that was one of his lifetimes ago.

'What I particularly admire, if you'll allow me to say so, is that you switched so fast when you had to.'

I didn't understand this at all.

'Yeah,' I said. 'Though it hurt. I'd have liked to clear up Buxton.'

'That's a reporter's job, not an analyst's. But the Volunteers now: that's business.'

I almost gaped at him, but if I had he wouldn't have noticed. He was so generally wide awake that he noticed very little within touching distance.

'It might be,' I said.

He gave me his smile – his seniority smile.

'You'll kill me, Lewis, but I broke your lock.'

'Yeah?'

'I also got on the line to New York. We broke Jacobs's lock too.'

'Thanks,' I said. I now at least understood the smile. Senior analysts have the right to appeal to Regional or Network Controllers to break any lock on an ordinary analyst's or reporter's material. It's their safeguard, they say, in allowing the procedure at all.

'It's big, Lewis,' he said, still smiling. 'The biggest in years. Jacobs, of course, gets some of the credit. Through his little pick-up in Washington. But we're agreed at our level: it was you really started it.'

'What, PRC funding Evans's Trust?'

'Well that was just the lead. I mean it's obviously true but who cares? Some petty liberal outfit has been on the take: well they all are, aren't they, one way or the other? Whereas the Volunteers, that's the big one. We've cleared a whole section, we have all the priorities. The Volunteers, as of now, is the name of the game.'

'Game is right,' I said.

He chose to ignore this. 'I've been through all your material, Lewis. The Mark Evans cover, the telebiography, that was a very bright thing to do.'

Yeah, bright.

'Your own brief, now, follows perfectly from that. You zoom in on Evans. You go all out to break him.'

'That's from Jacobs, is it?'

'Yes of course, you've not seen that part of his stuff. But sure, straight up. Evans is dead centre. Over here, that is. And what we're trying to get is at least the major network.'

'As a news item?' I said, pitching the irony low.

'Item! My God, this will stop the tapes. In fifteen countries – that's Pete Jacobs's estimate – a conscious organisation to infiltrate the establishment: the civil service, the army, the police, the banks.'

'The corporations,' I added, but he was in spate.

'And they're in there already, you realise that, Lewis? I mean most of them junior but on their safe way up. And why didn't it happen before, that's all I keep asking. At the moment in history when the State became the Problem, the modern managerial State, where else, for God's sake, would any serious radical go?'

'They've been trying for years. Since the Fabians,' I said.

'Yes but the Fabians were open about it. Their whole line was gradual persuasion. This is quite different. This is conscious occupation of the critical centres of power. And not for persuasion, Lewis. For takeover.'

'So you get another State. A volunteer autocracy.'

'No, no. You must read Pete Jacobs's stuff. These are radicals, Lewis; they mean to change the whole system.'

'Don't we all?' I said, looking away.

'We all did,' Friedmann said, and that was a laugh. 'But it's so obvious now, once this new way's been found. All the old stuff is out; the petty demonstrations, the radical playgroups, the polite social criticism, the party games, the manifestos. As if, for God's sake, this was an open society, like in its own rhetoric. When the reality, always, is this simple control: of the force and of the money.'

'You'll persuade me,' I said. 'I'll volunteer myself.'

He gave me the nicest possible laugh. 'You're known,' he said, sweetly.

'Yes indeed. I'm known because I am.'

'That's Descartes, isn't it?' he said in a hurry.

'Translated,' I said. 'But all I'm asking, really, is why these people should change the system when they've become the system.'

'Because they're dedicated, Lewis.'

'I see. So we bust them?'

Something crossed his face. It might have been anything: fear, shame, conscience; intelligence even, putting two and two together.

'Bust them, Lewis? Good Lord, no. We're a news operation, not a security service. We just report the facts.'

'On a secret operation?'

'That's a problem, I admit. But not our problem, Lewis.'

'It will become our problem. We give the story, we give the names. Then all hell will break loose. They'll be out on their arses.'

'I doubt it,' he said. 'They've been covering their tracks.'

'Yes. Like we name Mark Evans and Gridfile runs every public servant he's given a reference for, even met at a party. And no chances will be taken; they'll all be out.'

'On what grounds, Lewis? On what provable grounds?'

'Well,' I said, 'if control's that simple, if it's only force and money, they won't need any grounds. All the witches will simply be burned.'

'I doubt it,' he said. 'These are clever people. But anyway, Lewis, it's out of our hands. It's on its way to public property, whatever we think about it.'

'Some of it is.'

'Well in any case, Lewis, you started it, didn't you? If publicity is a problem, it's a rather personal problem for you.'

3

I hadn't needed that last observation. I had got to it already. So that by current ethics I was almost home and dry. I knew my fault; I knew my capacity for self-deception; I knew the pettiness of the soul. All that remained, really, was the usual piquant self-disgust, which I would generously, even insistently, offer to share with everyone else, until it became a culture.

But I've got shy of current ethics. I prefer having to do something. And what I now had to do was, by any standard, sufficiently difficult, sufficiently complex, to need all my energy and attention.

Not that the technicalities were difficult. Friedmann had assigned me, full time, to Mark Evans: 'to zoom in and break him', of course on the Volunteers. The fact that beyond ordinary curiosity I didn't give a damn about these official volunteers didn't mean that I wasn't going where I wanted to go. A gap had opened between work and intention, but by chance, it seemed, their occasions coincided. All I really wanted to know was who had shot Buxton and why, and its real connections with the only important event in this whole sequence: the killing of Gareth Powell at Pontyrhiw.

I went back to the flat and locked myself in. I had to resist, for twenty-four hours at least, every impulse I had learned in what could be called my training, my work experience – every impulse, that is, to make phone calls, contact people, inquire within and without. Most of the mistakes I had made had been a direct consequence of this get-up-and-go, so what I now had to do was stay still and look at it all, past all the usual stages in which idleness and habit combine to conclude that we have looked long enough and that it has at last come clear.

I don't think I got there, though I got some of the way. A dozen times, at least, I got up and said 'that's it', though it wasn't. As often, I suppose, I reached an emotional state which appeared to be a solution. The compounding of my faults in the faults of everyone else; a cheerful and then a bitter cynicism. Or else a cold abstraction, in which I saw everything structurally or historically, myself as a carrier, an agent, a symptom among others – a lovely dreamy state that, the cool, analytic and alienated intelligence. Disgust, of course, which is cheap these days, the raw material being so plentiful. Then anger, even hatred, especially a hatred of Buxton. That lasted longer than the others. But an emotional state is not a conclusion; that's where literature stopped, a few decades ago.

I then fell asleep in my clothes. I slept for ten hours: longer than in years. When I woke it was clear that I was going back to Wales: one of the lines that had emerged in the previous day's chaos. I had spent some of the time re-reading all my notes on Evans, with the advantage, of course, that I now knew where he had ended, with the PRC Trust and the organised Volunteers. And it kept staring at me, a blank stare: the end of his first marriage, the first wife, the two sons. There, after all, something fundamental had happened, or at least had been registered. In our instant society we take, we have to, most people as they come. Their past, their history, if we care about it at all, is on the record but no more: it doesn't really connect with their more apparently relevant present. But this had been twenty-one years of his life: a marriage and two sons, now twenty-five and twenty-four. I wanted to see Joan Evans. I wanted to see the sons, David and Evan. This can be put down now as reporter's luck, but I'm telling it as it happened. I got a car and made for the motorway. In four hours I was in Llanmawnog.

I parked the car in a lane and stood looking across at Llanmawnog Hall. It is a beautiful old stone farmhouse, with massive round pillars in its sandstone barn. A settled place, with its sheltering pines and larches. Trimmed hedges of hazel and hawthorn, wild roses and honeysuckle growing through them everywhere, and an abundance of foxgloves in the banks. Stone posts for the gates: massive upended stones, like menhirs, but drilled for hinges and bolts. The track from the road, past a windbreak of hollies, was worn into the land, like a natural feature.

It was late afternoon. I had watched Joan Evans drive back from school. A young, red-haired man was working in the orchard at the side of the house: slashing brambles in an overgrown corner. I got the car and drove up.

Joan Evans answered the front door. She had to unbolt it at top and bottom, while I realised my mistake: I should of course have gone round the back. But she greeted me pleasantly. A handsome, plumping, sunburned woman: thin sandy hair, light blue eyes, freckled. Her voice high-pitched, rather fast. I explained and apologised. I was working on a telebiography of her former husband. I was in the district and wanted very much to talk to her.

'You'd better come in, Mr... ?'

'Redfern.'

'Mr Redfern. Come on in. Only I've just got back from school. Nothing's tidy anywhere.'

She led me into a long sitting room on the south of the house. We sat in chairs placed to look out over the orchard and through a gap in the woods to one of the whaleback hills.

'What a lovely place,' I said, meaning it. 'How could he ever bear to leave it?'

'Many of us have to, Mr Redfern. Nothing gets settled down here.'

'Well I was just thinking it was wonderfully settled.'

'You're playing on the word. That's not fair. Mark went up to Parliament because this country is dying. Whether it's here, in the fields, or over the top, in the valleys, it's the same really: we're a deprived country.'

I didn't look at her while she was saying this, I examined the view as if I needed to memorise it. I could see that she believed every word she said, but for someone like her, in a culture like that, belief is not a problem, in the way it is for the rest of us. The believing had been done for her; she had only to assent and live with its forms.

'It didn't work out,' I said, awkwardly.

'How could it work out? But it had to be done.'

She was beginning to unnerve me.

'When did you come to live in this house, Mrs Evans?'

'In 1968. When Mark got his directorship in Brecon. And he'd been adopted for this constituency.'

'Where had you lived before?'

'Tredegar, since we were married.'

'This must have been an improvement.'

'It was lovely. The boys loved it. And Mark, you see, had just completed Stage One of his work. His book was the

175

culmination of those years in the Labour Colleges. Now Stage Two had to start.'

'He put it like that?'

'We saw it like that. We discussed it together.'

'Including the paradox, I suppose, that having written his book about the limits of representative democracy, he was preparing to step inside them.'

She smiled with great assurance. 'Oh that,' she said. 'Of course we saw that. But Mark knew what he was doing.'

'What was he doing?'

'Well, Mr Redfern, when you have recognised the limits, you approach them and push them back.'

'Is that what he said?'

'It's what we both said.'

'But then it didn't happen.'

'What do you mean, Mr Redfern? It did happen. Mark took it right on, through Stage Two. Did you not read his new preface?'

'That was an advance, certainly. But it was also, wasn't it, a kind of apology, a confession? A confession of failure.'

'Mark? A failure?'

'But you must have felt it yourself. Because during this process your marriage ended.'

'Yes, Redfern, it did.' She flushed slightly. The freckles seemed suddenly lighter. But she didn't move or look away.

'Don't tell me that was Stage Three.'

She looked at me steadily. It was as if she was thinking over what one of her more awkward pupils had come out with. But there was then an interruption. The door was flung open, and the young man who had been in the orchard stood looking in at us. He was in his mid-twenties: red-haired, broad-shouldered; sweating through his shirt.

176

'Evan.'

'Hullo.'

'This is Mr Redfern. He's come to talk about Dad.'

Evan nodded and went out. His mother's eyes followed him.

'He's just back from Africa. On three months leave. He's a geologist working for the East Africa Federation.'

'Your younger son?'

'Yes.'

'And your other son?'

'David? Oh he's a librarian in London.'

I again set to work on the view. I was silent for so long that she had to make a new move.

'Was there anything particular, Mr Redfern, I could tell you about Mark?'

'You see my difficulty, Mrs Evans. It isn't my business to pry into private affairs. But let me put it this way. I'm saying, on what I know, that Mark Evans changed, when he was elected and went to London. The man you describe would of course have to change. He wouldn't be pushing the limits, they'd be pushing him. And he'd think he could solve this by saying so, or by talking about stages. But then, after all, in the most central way, he saw himself differently. He made a different kind of life.'

'We both knew it would be different.'

'Not that different. You surely never foresaw that?'

'Foresaw what, Mr Redfern?'

'I meant the divorce.'

'Yes.'

'I meant Mrs Praager.'

'Yes, I know you did, Mr Redfern.'

'You don't think he changed then?'

'Our marriage changed, Mr Redfern. There's no secret about that.'

'Your marriage ended, Mrs Evans.'

'Changed and then ended. That was my decision.'

'For his sake, do you mean?'

'No, not entirely. It was the right thing for both of us.'

'Because it had ended?'

'Because it had changed.'

I waited for some moments. Then I asked my real question. 'Did you see him at all afterwards?'

'At times, yes.'

'He visited your sons?'

'Oh yes, regularly.'

'And visited you?'

'Yes. Occasionally.'

Her face was still quite calm. 'You see,' she went on, 'his mother lives in Llanmawnog. When he visited her, we would sometimes meet.'

'On good terms?'

'On different terms. But you could say they were good.'

The phrase was too rehearsed. She was playing it now as an interview. But then, what else?

The door was pushed open, again roughly. Evan came in with a tray of tea. He put it down in front of his mother. Then he looked across at me.

'Won't you stay and have your tea in here, Evan?' his mother asked. She had noticed, as I had, that there were only two cups on the tray.

'No, I've had mine. I'll get out and burn up that stuff.'

'We're talking about your Dad. Mr Redfern is a reporter.'

'Who for?' Evan asked.

'Insatel.'

He breathed down hard through his nose. One of the simpler forms of dissent.

'You see us in East Africa?'

'The tin gods of the open sky,' he said, as if to the view. His voice was rough, with a very marked Welsh accent.

'Is that how we look?'

'You have nothing to say for us. You have plenty to say *to* us. You beam in from another world.'

'And local stations can't compete. Is that the real trouble? That people prefer Insatel.'

'Most people prefer what's cheap. If you're very poor it's not even a choice.'

'Yes, I know the argument. We fight it out all the time, inside the organisation.'

'Let us know when you win,' he said roughly. Then he turned and went out.

His mother's eyes followed him. I wondered what she would say.

'He's so like Mark,' she said, astonishing me. 'Not to look at, of course. But in how he sees the world: very hard and no compromise.'

'At that age, perhaps.'

'At that age, of course, but then on through his life.'

I sipped my tea. 'I mustn't keep you much longer,' I said, pushing her. 'Mark came down, didn't he, for the Pontyrhiw Memorial? Did you happen to discuss that with him?'

'Yes, of course. But he felt as we all did. And he was getting his Trust to help.'

This was news, but it wasn't what I wanted.

'He came up here after the Memorial?'

'Yes, on the Monday.'

'And went back to London that night?'

'Yes.'

'You don't happen to know what train he was catching. It's an odd thing to ask, but he may have been in time to see a man I want to contact, if in fact...'

I was getting deeper and deeper into this covering story, but she wasn't interested. She just answered my question.

'The 8.10 from Cardiff.'

'I see.'

'He'd been to his mother before he came to see us. He drove straight from here to the station.'

'How long does it take, by the way? To drive down to Cardiff.'

'About an hour and a half. He left at half-past six.'

So there it was. Safely on the road, between Llanmawnog and Cardiff, while Buxton was being shot at St Fagans. That disposed of one of my simpler suppositions.

There was then nothing more to get. But because I found myself respecting her, I went through with the routine. I asked for photographs of different periods in his life. She got them at once; they were all carefully preserved and arranged. I promised to copy and return them. Actually, as I saw them, they interested me. It is always strange to see a face developing, and certainly this face, until his late thirties, was interesting: strong, hard, aggressive, impatient – the face I had briefly glimpsed in his office. Then, through his forties, it composed and settled, became merely distinguished: or was it just that then I knew it?

I took other scraps. She was so persistently kind. It had been a real marriage evidently: substantial, settled and fertile. What kind of fool had he been to run out on that? It made the earlier man seem much better than I had thought and then, of course, inevitably, made the later man much worse. But that regularity is too dismal. It is put there to make us give up.

I took my leave politely. As I was starting the car there was a huge leaping bonfire in the orchard: Evan burning the cut rubbish. He took no notice of my going. He had his work.

4

As I drove back I kept breathing out hard. It took me a long time to settle. It was twenty miles before I got to a road I could relax on: not just wider and straighter, though that helped, but a road of my own world, a road of long-range mobility, within a large social network, rather than the insistently local and settled lines that I was leaving. I drove hard, once I was really out again. The work experience began to take over. Thinking of office hours, I stopped at a service area and called the Library Association. When I drove on I had the address of David Evans's library. I would be there before they opened in the morning.

He was easy to recognise. Tall, fair, with an obvious facial resemblance to his father. I got a decent photograph of him, from the car I'd parked near the entrance. Within the hour I was down at Rentaday, where I'd taken the trouble to hire my own car: these continuities help. I spoke to the girl I'd spoken to before, who'd rented the car to the supposed J. Tiller. She remembered my previous inquiry, when I'd shown her the other photographs. I talked to her longer than I needed. I was still in two minds whether to show her the new photograph: it was very likely that she would recognise it but if she did what happened next, if the police checked back with her?

In the end there was only one way. We had lunch at the pub round the corner. The Llandaff car, I explained, had now been eliminated from the police investigation. That was why,

I said – risking my luck, and winning – the police had never been back to her. But it was important in something else: in fact, would you believe it, in an elopement? She believed it. She accepted my condition that it had to be kept very private. We saw eye to eye about the importance of private life. After that, after all that, the showing of the photograph was just a formality. She recognised it. She recognised David Evans as the young man, the German student, who had hired the car to go to Wales. Yes, I told her, he was a German student, though his name wasn't Tiller; it was Krenek. And it was very romantic: he and this Welsh girl, married to a much older man, had got away to Canada. I bit my lip on Canada, but I don't think she noticed. We finished lunch; I walked her back; I told her I would be in again, in a day or two, for a car. As I walked away I felt sick.

But the mechanics of the shooting of Buxton were now almost wholly explained. I had fulfilled my original assignment, though neither the police nor Insatel were any longer much interested. Yet I did what I had to do, as if the inquiry were still live. I checked back on David Evans. I was then surprised by one of those odd connections which had continually disturbed the apparently simple lines of this case. I now knew that he and Rosa had worked together at St Fagans, so I was expecting, with some confidence, records of previous contacts between them. What I got instead was the fact that David and *Sarah* had been contemporaries at Cambridge – in fact in the same college and reading the same subject. So that Mark Evans's son and the girl who was now his second wife had been at least that close, just five or six years back. That turned me right off, for some hours. I would prefer to think better of people.

So, I imagined, would David Evans. For that in the end

was how I saw it. Thinking over the ways in which I could try to confirm it, I decided to ring Rosa. We talked business for some time. Then, when I was winding up, I said casually: 'By the way, when we were talking about the father, you didn't mention the son.'

'What son?' she said, surprised.

'David.'

There was a considerable silence. I could imagine her grey cheeks.

'Though you were with him in Wales.'

'Have you gone back to that?' she eventually asked.

'Back? I've never left it.'

She put down the phone. That was a mistake, obviously, but probably I, too, had made a mistake. But I didn't now much care. Every strategy had collapsed, and I was left, at best, with tactics. Let someone else move, for a change.

5

They moved fast, and together, at least in time. I got a call from Mark Evans's secretary, asking me to come in that evening to see him: at his office, about nine. I had only just agreed when I got a call from Rosa.

'We're coming round tonight.'

'We?'

'Bill and David and I.'

'Not Lucy?'

'No, she's gone.'

I waited a few moments.

'Well, it's no use tonight. I shan't be here, I'll be working.'

'Till when?'

'Oh midnight, I expect. Why not come another time?'

'No, it's moving too fast. It has to be tonight.'

'Well I've told you, I shan't be here.'

'We'll wait.'

'Outside? You'll get bored.'

'Well yes, you do bore us. But we'll wait.'

'It's your choice,' I said, and rang off.

I made a few preparations before I left the flat. Strangely enough, all my energy was back, now that the others were moving. I can always respond; it's moving on my own I find difficult.

I had a good meal before I went to see Evans. I wanted some kind of assurance to match his office. When I got to the building it was locked. I rang the bell, and his voice answered me: 'Who?' 'Redfern,' I said, as clipped as his machine. 'Come,' he said, and the lock was released. I went up, by the stairs; the lift wasn't working.

I tapped at the door of his office. There was quite a long delay, but then he was there, with his jacket off, wearing a black jersey. The gracious office was not lighted, except for the lamps from the street.

'I'm through here,' he said, and led the way through the office to a door in the corner. There was a very small room beyond it, with just a desk and typewriter, two chairs and books.

'This is where I work.'

'And out there?'

'Meet people.'

'Yes,' I said, 'we've met.'

He sat on the chair by the desk. He pointed me into the other. All his movements, now, were sharp and controlled, and his voice was different: much harder, less persuasive.

'I asked you to come because it's time to be frank. You set up this story of a telebiography. Set it up quite carefully. I've checked with your company.'

'Who are always frank.'

'Look, I've had my run of hostility. If it was just the usual sour piece – the public failure, the fallen idol – I'd have taken it. I'd have taken an hour of it for five minutes to speak as myself.'

'Don't you ever watch us? Don't you know who does the talking?'

'It doesn't matter. That's behind us now. There will be no programme.'

'Don't rely on that, Mr Evans.'

186

'Yes, your programme was a cover. But then the obvious question is a cover for what? When you last came to see me I thought I'd got the answer. You would expose the Trust, publish this story of the funding by PRC.'

'I could. But my bosses don't think it's important. Shall I tell you what they said: that some petty liberal outfit has been on the take – well they all are, aren't they, one way or the other?'

He went stiff with anger. It was probably the 'petty' that did it. I could see that face of the younger photographs: hard, biting, aggressive.

'But even that squalid motive is too generous an estimate. I think your real assignment is the shooting of Buxton.'

'Not shooting Buxton, actually. Finding out who shot him.'

'And for some extraordinary reason you are trying to link me with that.'

'Was it your son told you this?'

'My son? Well yes he told me about your intrusion at Llanmawnog.'

'Which son?'

'My son Evan. He would have turned you out, if it had been left to him. But my wife, my former wife, is so naturally trusting and kind that she didn't see it, didn't see you as Evan at once saw you.'

'And how was that?' I asked.

'As complacent scum, I think was his phrase. Well?' he said sharply, as the silence prolonged itself. 'Have you nothing to say? No defence or explanation?'

'If you want the explanation you can have it,' I said. 'Yes, I've been working on the attack on Buxton. In fact I've cleared it up. I know who did it and how.'

'You'd obviously claim that. But what possible connection can it have with me?'

'Well you remember I asked you which son.'

'What has that to do with it?'

'And also I followed one of the attackers to your flat.'

He spread his hands on the edge of his desk, looking down at his fingers. 'You're not naming names. May I ask why?'

'Because they don't matter. I know the whole story, but I shan't be reporting it. I shan't even be asked to report it.'

'That's difficult to believe.'

'Yes, scum is much easier to say.'

'But what reason can you have? This is a police matter.'

'I know. But I'm not the police.'

'You're a reporter, though. And it would be your story. A sensational story.'

'Yes. Yes it would. But you have to understand the complexities of news. It would be a big story, if I chose to tell it. But as I said I shan't be asked. Because now there's a bigger story.'

'The Trust? Surely not?'

'Not the Trust. Not its funding, Not even your cover-up inquiry.'

'What then?' he asked, watching we.

'The Volunteers,' I said.

'I don't know what you mean.'

'Look, your word for this talk was frank. You thought you'd call me in for this ritual accusation. You'd expose my deceptions, turn the hosepipe on me, let me crawl away to die. But you've no idea of the real situation. No idea, even now, of your danger.'

'*My* danger?'

'I was taken off Buxton. I was told to forget the Trust.

Would you like me to tell you my actual instructions? To zoom in on you, to break you. On this bigger story, that the whole network's after. The story that cancels the others. The Volunteers.'

He looked carefully across at me. 'Is that why you came then? Came tonight?'

'No, it's not why I came. I came to warn you. If you can stop being indignant and just listen for a while.'

He thought for some time.

'You've not made it easy to trust you, Mr Redfern.'

'No, I see that. I can also imagine my employers saying it.'

'Yes, you're experienced, of course, in a particular world. And just because you're experienced, well, to be frank again, there are many methods of, what did you say, zooming in, breaking? Including, I take it, winning your victim's confidence, his trust, even in so obvious a way as offering to betray your employers.'

'That's all very well, but you haven't time to find out. This is an action just breaking. I don't know if I can hold it. I don't know if anyone can hold it.'

'Hold what exactly?'

'You've been directly named, as a key to this organisation. They have other names. They're working on them all. When they've got a bit further the whole story will break. And I don't need to tell you what will happen then.'

'Yes, you do need to tell me.'

'Well, when Insatel breaks this, the witch-hunt will start. And that won't be reporters or consultant analysts. It'll be the hard stuff.'

'Yes,' he said, 'I imagine it will.'

He put his hands on the desk. He seemed almost relaxed.

'Well, thank you, Mr Redfern,' he said and got up.

I couldn't match his movement. It was so unexpected. I could admire his self-possession but I wanted to get hold of him and shake him, shout the danger in his face.

'It's all right,' he said. 'I have delayed reactions. They're often mistaken for passivity.'

'Or for a wise calm.'

'That too,' he said, smiling.

'And in any case I suppose there's nothing to be done. Nothing but brace yourself for the storm.'

'We'll have to see,' he said.

I now managed to get up. He moved to lead me to the door.

'By the way,' he said as he passed me, 'you're not the only reporter assigned to this, I take it? I mean, in this country?'

'I told you, this is a priority story.'

'Yes. Yes of course. Who was it named me, by the way?'

'It was someone in Washington, I don't know the name.'

'I see. Yes. These rumours start everywhere, don't they?'

He was standing very close to me. He smiled. I moved to the door, and into the dim outer office. He walked beside me, seeing me politely, or safely, to the door.

'Just one thing before you go,' he said as we walked down the stairs. 'You research a lot of people. At least it's called research. It's an interesting process. We even tried it on you.'

'Don't rely on my past,' I said, irritably.

'No,' he said, laughing, 'there was never any danger of that. But it's interesting. It's especially interesting when the present connects.'

We had got to the door.

'I'm not the problem,' I said, stubbornly.

He smiled and let me out into the street.

6

I went for a drink before travelling back. I took three quick whiskies, in a crowded, noisy pub. People came there, presumably, to forget their own worlds. I wished, without hope, that I could forget mine. Though I had done all I could, and it had gone as I had planned, I was much more disturbed than I would have thought possible. It wasn't just the denunciation, though more of that had got through than I would have thought likely, after my quite long practice at taking it. 'Complacent scum', Evan had said. I remembered Lucy saying 'You're filthy'.

But the real disturbance was much more than that. I was still, in my mind, with Mark Evans on the stairs, when the claim on my allegiance had been so indirectly, so subtly, made. It wouldn't have mattered if I hadn't felt myself acknowledging it, felt the old pull to the people under attack. I could have gone from that door with a list of shared jobs: letting other people know, getting them to take their precautions; alerting friends, comrades, to the danger that was coming. And all that, of course, was the one last thing I could never now do, never even be considered to be allowed to do.

I kept telling myself that I had done what I could: I had alerted Evans. I kept also telling myself that it wasn't my organisation, they weren't my comrades, I didn't even agree with them, in theory or in practice. But it wasn't enough.

The feelings were more general. I wanted the cement that keeps so many lives together: the experience of belonging to something, of confirming an identity in the identification with others. And I hadn't got it, and I wasn't going to get it. On the contrary, when I got back to the flat I would find another group, but a group against me, a group living these same feelings as they came to deal with their enemy.

They were sitting in a car just along from my entrance: at least, two of them were, Rosa and Bill Chaney. Rosa got out when she saw me and came forward and stood there, in her usual take-it-or-leave-it way.

'You waited then?'

She didn't answer. Chaney got out behind her; he seemed embarrassed and nervous. He was looking towards the front door to the flats, and I followed his look. The door was just opening, and someone was coming out. When he got into the light I saw that it was David Evans. He walked quickly towards us.

'I'm David Evans. Hullo.'

We shook hands. I was comparing him, physically, with his father. He was taller, slimmer, with much fairer hair, but there was the same vibrant force. The face was narrower and much harder: the expression sharper, more questioning, than even the photographs of the young Mark. Chaney, meanwhile, was still twisting with nervousness. Rosa just passively stood there.

'I just slipped up to see if you were in,' David said, smiling.

It's always interesting to begin a relationship with a lie. There was no legal or at least normal way in which he could have got past that front door after dusk, when the security lock goes on and can be released only by a key or by one of the occupants of the flats.

'You made sure, I hope?'

'Sure. So shall we go up?'

'After you,' I said to Rosa.

She looked contemptuously across at me and made Chaney go first. I unlocked the door, and we trooped up the stairs. I went ahead into the flat and looked carefully around. Nothing was obviously out of place. The inspection had been professional, and that was another entry for the file.

We sat down. I gave them beer. David, evidently, was to be the spokesman.

'We've been impressed, Lewis, by your interest in Pontyrhiw and St Fagans.'

'Correctly linked,' I said, watching him.

'Exactly. But then we knew this would be so, by a comrade.'

I looked away at Rosa and Chaney. They weren't looking very comradely. Rosa was sullen and Chaney merely embarrassed.

'Just when did you decide that I was a comrade?'

'Decide? No, we didn't decide. We assumed it, we had to assume it. Because you must see, Lewis, everything depends on us assuming it. I mean if it weren't true it would be all very ugly. You must see that.'

'Sure,' I said, holding his look.

'And it was probably our fault, at an earlier stage, not to make more deliberate contact with you. I mean to share information, to discuss its implications. There were things you knew that we didn't, and perhaps the other way round. You could have helped us a great deal. But of course you still can.'

'There are gaps on both sides, that's obvious enough.'

'From both ends, you mean. We're not on different sides. But yes, sure, there are gaps. I mean we have no way of knowing what's happening now, in two quite relevant cases.'

'Insatel?'

'Indeed Insatel. And of course the police.'

'Which by definition I wouldn't know.'

'By definition, agreed. But perhaps indirectly?'

'Well,' I said, 'for Insatel it's over. If I wanted to broadcast the story, it wouldn't get on.'

'Why?' Rosa asked.

'It's not flattering, I'm afraid. Not when you've taken your kind of risk. But the Insatel conclusion I can report verbatim: "A minor Minister gets a few pellets in his calves. Christ, when you think of the world."'

'It wasn't done to impress *them*.'

'No', I agreed. 'It was done for Pontyrhiw.'

'Precisely,' Chaney said.

'Though of course without asking them,' I said, keeping to Rosa and Chaney. 'Their own response was of their own kind. This other, from the beginning, was a different strategy.'

David moved and took over again. 'It's reassuring, Lewis, what you say about Insatel. I mean, for example, it clarifies what we'd been assuming. About yourself, in the first place.'

'Sure.'

'However, there's still the police.'

'Who never close a file.'

'Of course. But it matters, wouldn't you say, whether it's a file or an active inquiry.'

'It's a file, I'd guess. There's hardly anyone still on it.'

'You've checked? Recently?'

'Sure I've checked. They're still going through the motions

but since the Tiller fiasco they've felt baffled, even let down. If they're still doing anything it will be in Wales: running the lists again, watching people.'

'That agrees with our information,' he said.

'That's it, then,' I said, as if ending the talk.

'No,' Rosa said, 'we're not leaving it at that.'

'What else can you do, except share your information? Or isn't that part of the deal?'

'There's no deal,' she said, bitterly.

David was trying to intervene when the telephone rang. I glanced at my watch. The call was exactly on time.

'Fine, no problems,' I told Bill Edwards, the duty editor at Insatel. 'But we'll stick to the schedule.'

Rosa and Bill were ignoring the call, but David was on to it at once. 'A precaution?' he asked, smiling.

'Sure.'

'What, regular calls, and if there's no reply there's a letter somewhere?'

'You've done this before,' I said. 'And by the way I'm not apologising. You took your own precautions.'

'Well it's good to look around, Lewis. Not that we've been too intrusive.'

'You want to check?' I said, standing up.

'The room's all right, but yes, sure, I'll check,' he said, surprising me.

He walked over and felt through my pockets and looked briefly at my watch. Then he took what looked like a calculator from his pocket and just held it between us. It was a nice, expensive West German model; it picks up any switched-on recorder within five metres.

'All the assumptions still holding,' he said, easily. He put the detector away.

'So?' I said.

'So you're a good reporter.'

'I could return the compliment. It's not my style, but you did a good job in *Death of a Loader*.'

'It was patched.'

He leaned back under the light. He had, I noticed, very thin, pale lips.

'Did Lucy blow Tiller?' I asked him.

'Yes. Sure. Her one service to politics.'

'Where did you get this right to patronise Lucy?'

'Okay, Lucy's straight. Mr Tiller, professional as he was, was not professional enough to understand a decent woman. Lucy minded very little about anything except that her friends should be honest and kind.'

'And exclusive,' Rosa said.

'Okay, exclusive. What's so wrong with that? What finished Lucy was Mr Tiller and a certain married lady. She went looking for that and found enough of the other. Of course she needed us to interpret it.'

As David talked, confidently, I was drawing away in my mind. For I thought I could see what was coming, and it wasn't so much that I didn't like it – if that was the criterion, I'd have to close my mind down – as that, if I was right, this was no way for him to be talking about it. I was trying to fit several other things together: the close, empathetic style of his Pontyrhiw pamphlet; the cool contempt of the St Fagans planning; the apparent ease of his handling of me. Face to face with David Evans I was a very long way, suddenly, behind my reputation. But I tried again.

'Tiller was working, of course, on the Volunteers?'

'Sure.'

'And on your father's involvement with them?'

'Yes.'

'So he went to Sarah?'

He sat up. He refilled his beer glass.

'They went to each other,' he said, half-smiling.

I looked quickly at Rosa. Her face was set and grey.

'You knew her well yourself,' I managed to say.

'Yes, that helped.'

'It must have been, at the least, very difficult for your father.'

'Oh he didn't know about Tiller. He still doesn't,' he added, with a hard emphasis.

'I didn't mean only that. I mean, as affecting you. The Volunteer note, for instance. Did you want to involve him?'

He put his glass down, hard, on the table. 'My father's dead, Lewis. You must know that.'

There were some moments of absolute silence. Rosa was staring at him, biting her lower lip. Even Chaney looked surprised. But David was quite unmoved.

'There are things even you don't know, Lewis. It was Rosa met my father, through work. Sarah, well, we all know smooth Sal. Then my father met her, through Rosa. He was already far down. He decided to die.'

'This is nonsense, David,' Rosa said angrily.

'No, love, it's the truth. Marrying Sarah was that: a familiar form of suicide. The man in his fifties, his project, his identity, collapsing inside and out. There's either death or disappearance: the orthodox fugue. Or there's this simpler cancellation. All the actual worn life is pushed aside. He marries a young woman as if, brightly hoping, he were still himself a young man: a young man with his project in front of him. And then it has, you see, to be someone like Sal. Someone empty enough to contain such a fantasy.'

The telephone rang again. I answered; it was Edwards. We confirmed the schedule.

'Look,' I said to David, 'I've just come from your father. And he isn't dead, he's still fighting for his life. And he's doing something with it, not much perhaps but enough.'

'The Volunteers? But that will blow any minute.'

'Yes and when it does you won't find him dead, you'll find him alive and being crucified.'

'That would do too,' he said, getting up.

'Oh for Christ's sake!'

'No,' he said. 'The Volunteers are a bonus. A few will survive, they might even be useful. But what matters is that the system will lose its confidence. Who can we trust, they'll all ask; and then they'll start wringing their hands. The enemy, they'll say, is within the gates. They'll start running this way and that, like a lot of frightened hens, and they'll suspect *everybody*. That's the bonus, Lewis. *Everybody*, including each other. And that can't be bad.'

'It will be bad for some good people.'

'Yeah. Sure. But they knew what they were doing. We all knew what we were doing. And these so-called Volunteers will have done one thing. The real volunteers will survive behind them, survive and carry on, through the very noise of this exposure.'

'That's hard, David.'

He stopped and looked seriously at me. 'Did you suppose something else?'

'No. I supposed it was hard, once I'd got past the tricks. But then tell me one thing. Why had Rosa to do it? Why not shoot Buxton yourself?'

'This is intolerable,' Rosa said. She had got up, angrily, and had pushed at Chaney.

'I only ask, David, because though you sound hard, it's always others doing things for you.'

'A volunteer is a volunteer,' he said, smiling.

The phone rang again, on the arranged diminishing interval. I didn't want to answer it. In the state I was in I didn't even much care if Edwards took alarm and got my letter opened. And I didn't want to break off, since they were obviously preparing to go.

'Better answer it, Lewis,' David said, quietly.

Rosa and Chaney were already near the door. I held David's look for some moments, then went to the phone. He waited to hear my reassuring answer, then nodded, smiled, and went quietly out.

There was another call that night, after I'd cancelled the schedule with Edwards. It was Mark Evans asking me to come and see him again. Not at the office, but the flat. He had something for me, he said. It would be one way of paying his debt.

It was very late, but of course I went. If I was on any side now it was probably his, though when I reflected this surprised me; I had got so used to being against him. Technically, even theoretically, I was with David and the others; it was their kind of harshness, I had always known, that I had turned, displaced, to my craft. But as it all worked through, and as I had no choice but to see it from outside, I could feel this other dimension, an experience I had every reason to know and understand: the experience, put simply, of failure, of what David had called the failure of a project, except that it was never only any single man's project; it was a generation, it was a history – an action that seemed ended and yet some way had still to be found; some way, all our ways.

I rang the bell at Mark's flat. I remembered watching Rosa arrive there; it seemed years back. And when I heard the voice, on the security lock, I was further confused. It was Sarah, of course, though for a moment it sounded like Rosa.

She opened the flat door to me. She was cool and smiling in a long jade-green dress. Mark was in the shadows beyond her: in a deep chair, surrounded by piles of papers, narrowly lit from an angled lamp.

'I can't get up,' he said as he saw me. 'I'm bound in by paper.'

'Sure.'

'But it's on its way out. I shall burn most of it.'

He was still working at high speed, sorting and discarding the papers. His face was flushed with the effort. It made him look younger and more active.

'Don't you find this with all writers, Mr Redfern?' Sarah said, conversationally. 'They're so centred on paper they build hoards of it around them. Or like those wasps that make nests out of paper, with just a small hole to get in and out.'

'It's all right, Sal,' Mark said. 'Lewis knows.'

'Knows what, darling?'

'Why I'm burning my papers.'

'Anybody,' I said, watching her, 'might have been glad to have them. The Nation. The Manuscript Fund. Even PRC.'

There was sweat on her upper lip. It was like porcelain sweating. 'I'll clear up in the kitchen,' she said and went out.

As the door closed behind her Mark got up. He took a long brown envelope from the space between the cushion and the arm of his chair.

'Put this in your pocket. Now,' he said.

'What is it?'

'Put it away. And hang on to it. You'll understand why.'

I took the envelope and folded it into an inside pocket. It was stiff and it crackled, like photocopy paper. He went back to his chair and went on sorting. Neither of us spoke for some time.

'Will you make it?' I finally asked.

'No, but we can limit the damage.'

'I heard a story about tapes. Recordings.'

'No. We record but then we erase.'

'Isn't that rather pointless?'

'Perhaps. But it's only symbolic anyway. I mean we'd have no hold, in any circumstances: no hold we could use, in good conscience. Whereas if other people got them...'

He went on sorting. I still thought of it as that though everything now seemed to be going for discard.

'Like harrowing the soul, would you say?' he asked, looking up at me.

'I've no experience. I suppose so.'

'I think you've had the experience. Perhaps not with piles of paper.'

'I don't know. I just feel puzzled. Everyone's treating me, suddenly, as a comrade-in-arms.'

He threw his head back and laughed. 'Well you've succeeded, haven't you? Succeeded quite brilliantly. An investigative triumph, whether you like it or not. But then don't, these last days, let go of your scepticism. You're popular now *because* you've succeeded. You're our comrade Success, whether we like you or not.'

I crossed and sat down. He was still half laughing at me, trying to share a laugh, after a mutual crisis, a mutual understanding. And this was all very well, except that I still felt outside it.

'I've been talking to David,' I said.

'Yes.'

'Do you still keep in touch with him?'

'With David? Not really. We quarrelled, very badly, when I married again. I see Evan, of course, whenever he's back.'

202

I had a long look, while he went on rapidly sorting, discarding, his papers. I didn't understand him. I couldn't focus him at all. The word that kept coming was mobile. I'd think I had him placed, or in two places even, and then he seemed somewhere else and a quite different man. Some trick, I would have supposed; some endless agility. At the beginning I had thought that: it had been his career, his politician's knack. But I was wondering now whether I'd ever had the eyes, whether what I was seeing, and squinting at, wasn't much larger, much more complex: the surprises not in him but, tellingly, for me. And just as I phrased that I remembered David, and exactly the same observation.

'I suppose you saw Rosa and David at Cardiff station,' I said. He didn't answer; didn't even look up. 'I mean the day Buxton was shot.'

He looked up quickly. 'You tell it, Lewis. It's your story.'

'Is it? It's nobody's story. Nobody wants it now.'

'It's still there though. It happened.'

'And happened to you.'

'Yes, to me. To a failed generation.'

'The sins of the fathers?'

'Not sins exactly. That's a dead language. But when you've tried all the ways, as I've tried all but one, and you've helped to build an opposition, an active force, and then you look at yourself, take the measure of your failure. Not a personal failure but a historical failure. The opposition is still opposition, the system is still there and you have not changed it. Then you start to see what must happen, the one last way. But what you contemplate as theory is suddenly practice, and your son is engaged in it, your son and your sons. A failed generation is contemptuously pushed aside. A new force emerges. A force that is strange to you but in it you can recognise your own features, your own language, your own being. Changed but connecting, father to son.'

'Then the sin was political failure,' I said, looking away.

'Of course it's political failure. We are rotten with failure, all of us rotten. You must know this. You particularly.'

'Yes,' I said. 'But if you think the alternative's that charade in the park...'

'I don't, Lewis. And neither do they. That too is a symptom of failure: a game and they know it.'

'Then what would success be?'

'You know what it must be. We have failed for one main reason, that our enemies are powerful. It's not first in ourselves, it's in them, in their force. And when you see that, you can't stick in dissent. You have only to attack them, by any means possible.'

'By violence, by deception?'

'By any means possible. That's where I've now got. And that I should be saying it, that's the point, Lewis, isn't it? That I, Mark Evans, should have got to that.'

'Yes,' I said. 'Yes. You're calling for volunteers.'

He got up suddenly. Several papers slipped to the floor. Sarah had come back and was standing in the doorway. She was watching him carefully, as if estimating a stranger.

'I must burn this stuff,' he said, quickly, looking down at the heaps of paper.

'Not tonight, Mark,' Sarah said, sharply.

'Tonight.'

He went out to the kitchen and came back with several black plastic dustbin bags. He squatted and began pushing the heaps of paper inside them.

'Can you?' I asked.

'There's a furnace in the basement.'

'The morning will do, Mark,' Sarah said.

'Tonight,' he said.

'Can I help?' I asked him.

'Yes, Lewis. Yes.'

Sarah turned angrily and went to her bedroom. I helped him stuff the last papers into the bags. We went out to the corridor and along to a service lift. As it made its slow way down he looked at me and said: 'Are you married, Lewis?'

'Yes and no. I'm married but separated. My wife's gone back to Canada.'

'Why?'

I smiled. He responded. How do questions like that get answered?

'She said I was two-faced.'

'Well you are, aren't you?' he said, still smiling.

'It's a way of putting it.'

'It's a kind way of putting it. She should have realised her luck. To be two-faced, now, is to be halfway pure. Most people go about with a score of faces.'

'But we remember the one we think we married.'

'We remember something, occasionally.'

The lift stopped. We carried the bags across to the furnace. He opened the plate and began feeding in the paper. It flared, and he paused, watching it curl and smoke before it caught fire.

'This envelope in my pocket,' I said.

He swung round sharply. 'Yes, don't for Christ's sake burn that.'

'What is it?'

He added another bundle to the leaping flames.

'It's Buxton's memorandum to the Cabinet, on Pontyrhiw. There's also the minutes of the Cabinet committee that took the decision.'

I said nothing. I was watching the flames. He went on feeding them, pushing the heaps of paper down angrily.

'From a Volunteer?' I asked.

'Don't worry. They're authentic.'

'So why do I get them?'

'You're a reporter, aren't you?'

'I can't report this. They would never let me do it.'

'I'm not asking you to report it. The public inquiry's still open. I've already asked John to request a special session, for new evidence to be presented.'

'Your brother? But then why not give these papers to him?'

'They must come from a neutral.'

'Which I still am?'

'Which you'll be taken as, Lewis.'

'With Cabinet papers? You know what will happen as soon as I've published them?'

'Yes. Yes, I know.'

'I'll be heavily interrogated, probably charged.'

'Almost certainly, yes. Their only other course would be to deny their authenticity. But if you present them at a public tribunal that's virtually impossible. The verification will be beyond challenge. And it will have become official evidence.'

'So I get interrogated?'

'Yes, Lewis. And you'll know what to say. That they came through the post, without indication of origin. Or that you know who handed them over but are bound by professional ethics to protect your sources.'

'Why should I do either?'

'Because you're involved, Lewis. And your reputation will help. It's well known you're not scrupulous.'

'I mean why should I be *willing* to do it?'

'Well, that's up to you.'

'I could take it out now and put it in the fire.'

He looked round again, making sure. He smiled.

'There are other copies, of course. In fact John's already received copies from you. At least they're in the post.'

I stared at him. 'What is this? Revenge, or blackmail?'

'Neither, surely.'

'You'd not get away with it.'

'We'd try. John trusts you. He thinks you're a radical reporter.'

'And you?'

'I think you're living your destiny, Lewis.'

'Volunteering for it, you mean?'

'If you want to say that. I'd say you were more a pressed man.'

'Pressed by you, you mean? Is this how you recruit?'

'No, basically pressed by yourself. I'm just, what do they call it, a providing agency.'

I went on staring at him. I was past assessment, past trying to understand him. The line between observer and participant, that I'd always theorised, had been turned so effortlessly. I'd broken secrets to him; I was helping him burn his compromising papers. And right in the middle of this shared and satisfying voluntary act I was turned, without hesitation, into another and much more difficult action. And not by his force, as he said. By my own momentum. By my own style.

'I'm getting out of this now,' I said.

He turned at once. He held out his hand. 'Well thank you for coming,' he said, as if he was still in his outer office. I even thought, ludicrously, that I was going away with a grant. 'Good luck,' he added.

I didn't take his hand. I was thinking of David and of the sins of the fathers. I wasn't going to shake hands on that. And another moment came back to me: when I had left his office, earlier that night, wishing, sentimentally, that I was still part of it all; that I was leaving, as a comrade, with my piece of shared work. Well, now I had it. It had been precisely selected for me and there was nothing comradely about it. My job, quite simply, was to do my job: to complete the inquiry on Buxton.

8

Friedmann had called a planning meeting for noon that day. I slept late, but I made it. It was a big affair: more than twenty people in the long office, with the high blinds filtering the sun. The fax-screen was on at one end of the room, where Friedmann could see it. He likes this sense of a racing world and himself just holding it on course. I leaned back from the table, tipping my chair. It was as near as I could get to dissociation, but the harder business was coming, and I was trying to gather my strength.

The Volunteers situation got worse every minute. As I heard the reports I felt myself shrinking. The American stuff was the worst. They'd identified the man who seemed to have started it: a man called Brown who'd been an engineer, who'd shot up inside two of the biggest corporations, who'd been taken on to Washington and into the top planning agency; for three years, during that, he'd been, among other things, on the board above PRC. And then something had happened to him. It was explained with the usual reductive simplicity, the appropriate crudeness of our times. He'd got divorced and remarried; the new wife was a liberal but more important very rich. The career man, suddenly, had an immense independence and at just the same time he had decided – we all smiled round the table – that the system he knew inside out was corrupt, that it was against the people, that it was against the future, and that in all its intricate and interlocking power it could never be broken by any of the old means but only from inside it, after long and careful penetration, specifically by the recruitment of thousands of volunteers.

Friedmann touched a switch. We saw a clip of Brown. But it might have been anybody: a government man, a corporation man: a voluntary corporation. I thought, watching it, of him talking to Mark Evans: passing the word, outlining the problem, delivering the solution.

It went on being bad news. Mike Davies had got a man who would talk: about how he'd been recruited, about his policy briefing, and of course now about his conscience. It couldn't have been much worse, except that he hadn't come in through Mark Evans – he'd never heard of him even – and still wouldn't name the man who'd recruited him. Also, I noticed, he insisted that there was only this one contact. There were other volunteers, probably even working beside him, but he didn't know who they were.

Then my own turn came. Yes, I'd seen Evans. In fact I'd practically spent the night with him. I'd zoomed in, as instructed, from at least three angles. But I hadn't broken him, I wasn't going to break him. He was very cool, very fly. It would all have to come from elsewhere.

It went as flat as it sounded. It was taken, with the usual politeness, more as my failure than as a fact about Evans, but I had to ride that. After the other reports they got on to timings. This was what I had to know: when the story would break. And that was a pleasant surprise. They were mostly so exalted with the size of the conspiracy that they all started saying they needed more time: that it was too big to be let out half-finished. And this, it turned out, was the line Friedmann had come to the meeting to sell. Priority and urgency, yes; premature disclosure, no. That meant at least a week: not enough, but something. And in any case it wasn't my job any more.

The meeting was breaking up when the message came on the screen:

SPECIAL SESSION PONTYRHIW RIOT INQUIRY AGREED EX UNION REQUEST QUOTE SENSATIONAL NEW EVIDENCE UNQUOTE.

Nobody took much notice. Most of them, I think, had already forgotten Pontyrhiw, or at least forgotten its importance, while 'sensational', which anywhere else might have attracted attention, is as commonplace in a news office as 'dear' at the beginning of a letter: neither means what it would elsewhere be taken to mean; only if it wasn't there might you look at it again.

Still, simple as it was, it had ended a whole sequence in my life. I had never thought it likely that Mark Evans was bluffing, but so many things go wrong in affairs like that, and I might have been rescued by some accident. Rescued, though, from what in myself, however reluctantly, I knew I must do. A condition of survival, in effect; of being able, from now on, to go on living with myself. But survival wasn't the most obvious word when what would actually happen was a form of self-destruction.

There was still one last slight chance and I went for it. I disengaged Friedmann from the usual group that formed around him.

'I have a problem,' I said. 'I want to come off this story, because the other has just come alight.'

'The other?' he said, as if nothing else had ever happened in human history.

'Pontyrhiw,' I said. 'Didn't you see the message?'

'Lewis, you were never on that Pontyrhiw business.'

'Well not directly, but from the Buxton shooting. It's the same affair, in effect.'

'I'll take your word for it, but I thought I'd made it clear: the Buxton thing is spiked.'

'On what you know at present. But I have this new material.'

'Showing what?' he asked, gesturing as he spoke for someone else to wait.

'Showing that Buxton gave the order for the army attack.' I was working very hard to keep my voice steady. I knew most of the pitfalls at just this point.

'So?' he said, sharply. 'Don't we all know that already?'

'Not as certainty, no.'

'And how would you prove certainty?'

'I have papers.'

'What papers?'

'Official papers.'

He was concentrating now. He had put on his hawk look. 'How official?'

'The best.'

'From?'

'From a contact.'

'I should have to know.'

'No. An intermediary.'

'I should have to know him.'

'You mean when you use it?'

'When I am deciding if we can use it.'

'And if you decided not, then...'

'Then I'd have decided not.'

'But you'd still have the name.'

212

It was time for the hawk to strike.

'Don't you trust me, Lewis?'

'It isn't that.'

'I don't mean trust me personally. I mean trust my position, which includes your position.'

'I hope I do.'

'Hope! Then what is it you're asking?'

'To give this evidence to the public inquiry. Which would be our plain duty, simultaneously with publishing.'

'You don't have to tell me that, Lewis.'

'You agree then?'

'I agree to consider it, when you've shown me it's genuine.'

'It verifies itself.'

'Not quite, Lewis. I would have to have the name.'

'You're making it very difficult for me.'

'No. The position makes it difficult. All I'm telling you, as you know, is just standard editorial practice.'

'I'll have to think about it,' I said. But I wasn't thinking about it. There was nothing to think about. All I was looking for, desperately, was some easy way out, and of course Friedmann wouldn't, indeed couldn't, provide this.

'Why,' he asked, 'if you already have the papers, do you want to go off your present assignment?'

'To get the stuff ready. To work on how to present it. It needs context, after all.'

'There'd be time for that. What's your actual reason?'

'There's no other.'

'Come on, Lewis, I can read. A special session of this inquiry has already been called, by the union. It's already been promised sensational evidence.'

'So?'

213

'So someone else already has it. Or knows where it is.'

'If it's the same. It could be something else.'

'It could be a list of the Kings of Israel but we both know it isn't. So what gives, Lewis? What's your positive reason?'

'For wanting to present it?'

'No, for wanting to drop out of the Volunteers story.'

'Did I say I wanted to drop out?'

'Yes, Lewis, you did.'

'As a matter of relative priority, that's all.'

'Because you can't crack Mark Evans?'

'Well that too, I suppose.'

'You go to Evans and you come back with nothing. But quite coincidentally you get a major break on something else.'

'Yes, coincidentally.'

'You're lying, Lewis. Where else would it come from? Isn't this, precisely, what these Volunteers are for?'

'Not by your account. I mean, by the account we've all had so far. Where they just beaver their way up.'

'Passing a document or two, meanwhile, on the side.'

'There's no evidence of that.'

He looked closely at me, smiling. 'What was the deal, Lewis? To lay off Evans, in return for the documents?'

'No. How could we lay off him?'

'We, perhaps. But you. And you matter.'

'Not now I don't.'

'You matter very much. Because the way I see it you've made another breakthrough. These documents give you some actual proof of how these Volunteers operate, the sort of thing they can do. So that you're not off the story; you must see that. You're on it and in it, all the way.'

'Meaning the papers don't bear on Buxton and Pontyrhiw,

but by a convenient shift back to the Volunteers?'

'They'll bear on both. On both, Lewis.'

I must have been looking dejected. Anyway I could see, in his face, that he knew he had won. So I had no option left; no option but to lose, as a way of defeating him.

'I'll put my resignation in the office,' I said.

He looked very surprised. He said the wrong thing.

'Don't threaten me, Lewis.'

'No threat. Just resignation.'

I turned and walked quickly away. I had begun to feel afraid. Only action could overcome that.

9

I typed and signed my resignation in the main office. I put it in an envelope and sealed it, addressed to Personnel. I then went out without depositing it. It may have been – who can tell? – some unconscious, last-minute reluctance, but something more immediate had occurred to me as I sealed it. Friedmann, I believed, was capable of anything, in what he saw as his work and his duty. He had not mentioned it, but I knew that on stories like this, for all the show of independence – the freedom of the air – it was policy to keep the State authorities informed, or at least to inform them before actual broadcast. Insatel, being para-national, might in theory have less obligation to do this, but in practice, given the strength of the lobby against para-nationals, which had been building very strongly since the Atticus affair, it was if anything more punctilious, more cautious, than even the domestic companies. So just now he had a problem. If I was really walking out with copies of Cabinet papers, which Insatel wouldn't even get to use, he might see the chance of a bargain, to gain some particular indulgence. Yet he would not do this, I thought, until he was sure that I had resigned: until the letter was there, in fact. We both knew, of course, how often the intention to resign is announced, in places like this, and how comparatively rarely it is gone through with; the unemployment figures are written in air between the anger and the act. It depended on the rest of his timing, but

I thought he would wait for the letter.

So I would let him wait. I would get clear of the flat, make arrangements about the papers, and only then post the letter. By second-class mail, I decided, laughing for a moment before the depression came down again and hit me: a depression at losing the job, of course; a related depression as I looked at the traps I had so cleverly walked into, Mark Evans's trap and Friedmann's; but then beyond these something much deeper, much more wasting: a perception of society, of my own society and of myself as its willing member, in which energy, intelligence, professional skills – all the virtues we are trained to – are so thoroughly enlisted in relationships which, at almost every level, involve calculation, indirection, half-truth, advantage. Certainly everybody says this about our society. It can be set up in permanent type in the entire opinion business. But nobody, in my book, means it, until he is, at some cost, walking steadily away from the world it describes. And if I now felt some strength, as I was actually walking away, and as the conventional words showed some prospect, for once, of an effective meaning, still, as I walked, I was calculating, assessing, preparing an indirection. And I could do nothing else, if I was really to get out.

I was out of the flat, with money, clothes and my passport, within an hour of leaving Friedmann. I then had some difficulty in devising a plan to safeguard the papers. I had to post them somewhere, to avoid them being found on me, but I no longer had the network and I couldn't involve any of the others I thought of: John Davies, David Evans, Rosa. Also Poste Restante I thought was too risky, if they really got after me; it's comparatively simple to circulate a name. In the end I decided on a small hotel in Malvern:

accessible from Wales but not too easily associated with it. I phoned and booked a room and then posted the papers to myself there. I had then only to make sure that I was not followed.

It was still like work; too much like work. And I was using the sense of emergency to suppress a more radical uncertainty. I had no real idea of the mechanics of the next decisive stage: the session of the Inquiry and my evidence at it. I got out of London first; I took a train to Bristol. I still had my resignation letter in my pocket. I took it out to post it but then put it back. I would first ring John Davies: indeed I ought to have done this much earlier.

He was out, and I had to wait. I put a coin in a seat-screen in the waiting room and watched Insatel; it was already tuned to it; seven out of ten are; for the sport, mainly. It was ordinary news, as if nothing was happening. A Brussels meeting came up: planes, suits, cars, flags, the facade of the office. And then suddenly there he was: Edmund Buxton; the Celtic sea negotiations. He was talking the usual crap, but I sat up and looked around, wanting everybody to listen to him, though of course nobody took any notice. I had to turn back and stare at him, on the small greasy screen, and I was breathing hard and my heart was thumping as he unreeled his negligible statement and the reporter's arm – Mr X's arm – stood respectfully at attention, holding the microphone, to amplify and record his slow temporising words. It was a release, suddenly: a release of pure anger, pure hate. I kept watching the arm as if it had been my own, and beyond it Buxton's face, with its settled rationality, its tired patience, its lined assumption of control. I could feel the seat around me and my body as part of it, and there was an intense concentration, an actual gathering of strength. I had my

218

mouth slightly open, my teeth parted, my fingers half clenched. As the clip finished I stood up quickly, and an entire world seemed to fall away. I left the screen running, let it go on playing to the empty seat. I could really walk away from it now.

I got through to John Davies. He was guarded, on the phone, but he said, rather formally, how much he and his colleagues appreciated my help, and that they would be glad to see me, whenever I could come, to discuss all the necessary arrangements. I said I would come straight over. He gave me an address, near the station. I posted the resignation letter and caught the first train. All my doubts had suddenly gone.

He was waiting for me at the house near the station. We stood in the back room, and he took my hand and again formally thanked me.

'I don't want to trouble you,' I said, 'but until next Wednesday I ought to stay somewhere quiet.'

'It's already fixed up, if it would suit,' he said.

For there was now suddenly a network again: to an indistinguishable house, in a terraced street, in a small town beyond Pontyrhiw. I could go there after dark, but I had still to recover the papers, from the hotel in Malvern. That was no bother, he assured me; I could borrow a car in the morning. There would be plenty of people who would help me.

'Like now you must consider,' he said, still formally, 'you've arrived among friends.'

10

It happened like that. I got the papers back but otherwise stayed in the house, in the front bedroom. John Davies and others came to see me, after dark always, and we sat in the bedroom and went through the evidence, planning the detailed presentation and trying to anticipate the inevitable cross-questions. Every detail was gone through, again and again, and we discussed the whole case as if our lives depended on it. As for me, I thought, it did, but this was never mentioned. If you're in a hard cause, you learn, you have to, a different ethics.

Then late on the Saturday night, after the usual visitors had gone, Mrs Probert came up and knocked and said Glyn, her son, had got a man by the door.

'We don't know him,' she said, 'but he's asking to see you.'

'He knows my name?'

'Yes, but he won't give his own. He just said to tell you he's come from St Fagans.'

I felt the jolt in my stomach, but I knew, from the style, who it was. I went to the landing and called down.

'David?'

He came forward into the light.

'You know him, Mr Redfern?' Glyn called up. He was there to guard the door, and in his shirt sleeves he looked as if he'd enjoy it.

'Yes, Glyn, thank you. He can come up.'

David Evans came up the stairs: moving lightly, vigorously, half-smiling. He took my hand as I stood in the door of my room and then closed the door firmly behind him.

'You're, wondering how I found you, Lewis.'

'Am I?'

'I just followed John Davies. I thought he must have you holed up. We got the rumour in London.'

'What rumour?'

'That you'd resigned from Insatel. That you'd come to the land of my fathers. And I bet they're looking after you. They need you, Lewis.'

'So I'm told.'

'The thing is – I know them much better than you – they think of this district as an enclave, its own little self-sufficient world. There's only, really, themselves and London, which they're usually fighting. So when you arrive from London, and appear to be on their side, they take you into their bosom, even hide you after a fashion, but forget how open and penetrable, open and penetrated, their place really is. They hide you but then visit you, only they come after dark as if nobody'd invented the headlamp.'

I asked him to sit down. I was tired and needed to sit down myself.

'You remind me of someone I know,' I said.

'Do I? Who?'

'Me. I talk like that. To avoid questions or just to postpone recognition.'

'Of course,' he said, and sat down. 'But nobody followed me, if that's what you're wondering. I'm not as strong as these people, but I have a much more developed sense of precaution. And it's necessary, Lewis. They're looking for

221

you all right.'

'Insatel?'

'Perhaps, but also the usual apes. They raided my father, by the way.'

'Christ, already?'

'It's all right. They're not really in touch. All they've got is from your Friedmann: this Volunteers caper.'

'But if I could connect it then they can.'

'No, Lewis. Not necessarily. You had special advantages, being a comrade. The advantages Insatel employed you for.'

'If you say so, David.'

'I do say so. But if you're thinking how clever you are –investigative grade one or any of that crap – you'll sink back now into this warm Welsh embrace, and the apes will bust you for certain. Your only hope, in fact, is to go on being your own particular kind of bastard.'

'Meaning?' I asked.

'Meaning watch the empathy, resume your professional scepticism. John Davies and his lads have welcomed you, haven't they, because you've got evidence and they want it presented. So they've taken you through it, been serious and helpful as far as the evidence goes. But I'll bet they've not mentioned what happens afterwards: what happens to you.'

'Your father made that clear.'

'Did he? Well, all right, he's lived in the world. But still you must know he doesn't give a damn. He never gives a damn. He's just his own project.'

I got a bottle and poured drinks. I needed both the whisky and the time.

'Then what?' I asked.

He looked up at me over his glass. He was watching me intently, with his staring blue eyes, but his face was still cold and distant: the voice and the manner quite separable.

'Do you want to get out? When you've given your evidence?'

'I've honestly not thought. I was trapped into this. Though by my own momentum.'

'I realise that. But you can't give up now. You must put in your evidence, we all want that, but you must also think beyond it. Don't psychologise it, that's all I'm saying.'

'Do you think that I am?'

'Sure. You've caught a heavy dose of guilt: about yourself, about your job, about whose side you've really been on. And you think exposure, punishment, is the painful but only cure.'

'No. I may have thought that. But the antidote came with it: that I could see I was being used, by your father, by...'

'You can say it, Lewis. By the movement down here.'

'All right but then I respect them. They're serving a true cause. They're avenging a death.'

'Sure. But still the problem is survival. The cause won't get far unless most of us survive.'

'I can be used again, if the State makes a case of it. The crusading reporter, we might even have a flag day.'

'That's better, Lewis. You're getting your moral sense back.'

'Does moral mean cynical?'

'Negativity, Lewis. You must have heard of it, you've lived it enough. But okay, if that's how you see it. It would be worth trying.'

'Of course they might not make a case of it. It's right in the grey. Between Cabinet papers, which are still theoretically publishable, and the Emergency Committee, which this was, and which, involving directions to the army...'

'Don't subtilise, Lewis. They make the rules. So you can be certain grey will be black.'

'Except for the political disadvantage. That the oftener it's tried, the more it discredits Buxton.'

'Discredit? Haven't you noticed what's happened to our charming public, since the screws went on? Most of them would shoot down anybody who causes them even temporary inconvenience. Or no, that's not fair. They'd get somebody else to shoot them.'

I emptied my glass. 'If that's true, David, what is any of this for?'

'What it was always for. To break the system that does that to people. To aggressor and victim alike.'

'And you still think we'll do it.'

'Of course we'll do it. In time.'

I got up. I walked to the window and looked out. The narrow street was empty. I could see the ridge of the hill beyond the houses opposite, a faint grey line against the summer night sky.

'Then I'll stay. What else can I do?'

'Well I could get you out. For six months or a year. Until the heat is off.'

'I've got my passport anyway.'

'You're very trusting, Lewis. If they move they'll move fast and play dirty. But even if they do we can arrange to move faster. You could be in Ireland or in France overnight.'

'I see. And then?'

'Well, you'd work. You have that right.'

'Not with a formal case against me.'

'Okay then, go further. Get out of the Community. You've got a wife in Canada, haven't you?'

'That's no use. We've split.'

'Since you worked for Insatel?'

'Since I worked for Insatel. Since I got this political assignment.'

'Yes, that's what I'd heard. Since you became their creep.'

'You know nothing about it.'

'It's what she said, Lewis.'

I jerked involuntarily. It was a moment of total surprise, total shock.

'You know her?' I asked.

'No, but we've made some inquiries. Since you started breathing down our necks. And we've let her know what's happening.'

'We?'

'We.'

I was feeling very tired. I wanted to flop on the bed, but I couldn't relax while he was still there.

'We were trying to understand you, Lewis,' he said quietly. He was speaking now with a low sibilant precision.

'No,' I said.

'We had what the comrades think is your history. Student militant in Birmingham. Three months gaol for assault on an industrial march. Reporter on the *Register* and *Swing*. Then straight from radical journalism to the job with Insatel.'

'Rocket,' I said.

'Megan told us other things. Only son of a widowed mother.'

'Exposed. Ambitious.'

'More than that, Lewis. Your father was killed as a soldier in Kenya. As a national service soldier. But in one of the very worst of the last colonial wars.'

I didn't answer for some moments. I avoided looking at him.

'He had no choice where he was sent.'

'Of course, Lewis. Imperialism killed him, whichever uniform he happened to be wearing. But you didn't think so. You told no one but Megan. You seemed bitterly ashamed.'

'Angry.'

'No, anger is public. You told none of your comrades. You wanted none of them to know. You let it fester under your exceptional activism. You divided yourself.'

'Now who's psychologising?' I protested.

'It's your political division that's important, Lewis. You told Megan the truth: not just the facts, the truth. You said you always suspected you were wearing the wrong uniform. That if the truth were ever known you would be seen as an impostor.'

'She left me,' I said.

'Not for that, Lewis. She tried hard to understand it. But do you remember when you told her? When you'd already accepted the job with Insatel, though you'd omitted to tell her that you'd even been asked.'

'It wasn't quite like that,' I protested.

'So when she heard of the job she thought – who wouldn't? – that it was an elaborate cover story. A play for sympathy, your unhappy childhood, to excuse a desertion.'

'All right, I remember the phrases.'

'She doesn't think that now.'

'How do you know what she thinks? All you've heard is self-justification.'

'She justified *you*, Lewis. When she heard about the Tribunal she said that was right, that it confirmed what she'd begun to believe. That you went into Insatel to use them. That when the right moment came you would simply walk out on them. That you'd wear their uniform but fight your own war.'

'A Volunteer, in fact,' I said, wrily.

He laughed.

'You and I, Lewis, know what to think about that.'

'You seem to.'

'And you seem to. You said, quite correctly, you were trapped.'

'By my own momentum.'

'And by calling your contradictions. He does that as a master.'

'Your father?'

'Yes. For don't forget, Lewis, I know this business about the uniforms we fight in. Within the same relationship.'

'If you say so, David.'

He got up. He looked across at me, then went to the window. 'All quiet in the valley,' he said, ironically.

'It's late.'

'I don't know. That's Maerdy up there, the street lights. If memories were battalions...'

I didn't answer. I was desperately tired.

'That's another thing Megan said. It's interesting. Both your parents' parents went from South Wales to Birmingham. In the thirties, to get work.'

'Yes.'

'So you're at the right distance to get this place wrong,' he said, turning and smiling.

'I got most of it right,' I said, quietly. 'From the beginning of this thing I got most of it right. More than anyone else I got most of it right.'

'Yes, Lewis. Virtually everything right. Virtually everything right but yourself.'

'So?'

'So I respect you for it. So it's the best way round.'

'Maybe,' I said.

He got ready to go.

'The help's there if you want it. Don't forget that, Lewis.'

'You mean, to get away?'

'Telling us two days before will do,' he said, zipping his jacket. I felt dull, staring at him.

'On a Wednesday France would be easier. You could go on from there.'

'Do you want me to go?'

'No, it's your decision. But if you mean to go it must be straight from the hearing. We'll take over from inside.'

'I'll think about it,' I said.

'But we shall need a message, if you're meaning to go.'

I was still staring at him. I was almost asleep on my feet. He went to the dressing table where there was a blue lace runner.

'Just hang this over the back of the mirror. By Monday mid-afternoon.'

'Is this necessary?' I asked.

'Yes, Lewis, believe me.'

11

The Inquiry hearing was in the Council Chamber at Llanedw, twenty miles from Pontyrhiw. It's policy to remove these affairs from the seat of the trouble, but twenty miles is now nothing and the whole building was crowded an hour before the session. I had been driven after breakfast to the union offices in the town. All the district committee were there, they told me. Actually there were so many people in the crowded offices it felt like the whole district. They were mostly men. They had put on tidy dark suits; most of them, even, were wearing collars and ties. I had nothing to match them: only the denim suit and the batik shirt I'd left in. I'd refused John Davies's offer to get me other clothes.

We were to arrive at the Chamber in a body. The cars were already drawn up, along the busy street, and when the time came we went down to them together, though there were then the usual arguments about who would ride with whom. My place was settled, however: in the back of the second car, with John Davies beside me. When we reached the Civic Centre there was a crowd outside, but there were stewards ready, alongside the police, and a way was cleared for us to go up the steps and inside. We moved along the corridor in a solid group. It was comforting, in a way, but I kept getting the feeling that I was literally being taken to court; that I was in a kind of custody. Beyond our immediate group, however, people were smiling and welcoming as we walked solidly through.

Our arrival was finely timed. We had just settled on our reserved seats when the Chairman entered and there was a command to stand. I looked round the crowded room. They were nearly all strangers. But then I saw a familiar face in the gallery: David Evans, smiling down. A girl with dark-brown hair was standing beside him. I had the feeling, looking up, that I had been trying to trace her, at Kilmichael Point. But I didn't know, of course. In fact I was certain of very little, any more. My world, my mobile world, had contracted to this point. Some rigmarole was being read, but I didn't listen to it. A man was standing behind David: his back turned, talking to someone behind him. Something else was said, and there was a noise of feet and chairs as we all moved to sit down. The man in the gallery turned. It was Mark Evans, cool and handsome in a white summer suit. I stared up at him, but he wasn't looking in my direction at all.

There were more formalities. John Davies was recalled and his formal request verified. I went on looking around the room. I saw only one more face I knew: square, reddish-skinned, with dark curly hair; the face resembling Gareth Powell's. It was that of his wife's brother, Bob, who had turned me out of her garden. I suppose I must have been staring at him because he caught my eye and smiled suddenly. I found myself smiling back and then, obscurely, felt angry.

The moment came, finally. I walked to the witness stand. I was moving automatically, but some emotion was running through me that I could not understand, could not even recognise. I say emotion, but that is too abstract. It was a physical condition: as of an intense otherness, an intense possession by otherness. My ordinary self seemed no more

230

than a bearer: a physical attendance, upon some other being and event.

Everyone was now looking at me. It was an extraordinary moment. I held my papers tightly and tried not to look back. On television, I suppose, I must have been watched by millions of people: watched, stared at. But it is entirely different. X marking the spot had now become the spot. I wanted, intensely, that they should not look.

Then the physical relations changed. There was counsel for the union: a man on his feet, a man speaking to me, and the others were fading.

'You are Lewis Redfern?'

'Yes.'

'You are a television reporter? With the Insatel organisation?'

'Yes.'

The Chairman interrupted. 'I understood, Mr Redfern, that you had left that employment.'

'Yes.'

'Then your answer to Mr Llewellyn was not strictly accurate.'

'It was accurate of the period when I obtained this evidence, sir.'

'Very well. But you are an educated man. You can distinguish, I take it, between a past and a present tense.'

'Yes.'

'We shall see. Go on.'

It was a bad start. I had forgotten the coldness of these practised procedures. And Llewellyn should not have let me in for it, though I could see why he had, to use Insatel's prestige. But it was late to think of that, to think of any of that.

231

It became simpler almost at once. Llewellyn took me, slowly and carefully, through the prepared ground. We were almost at the papers when the Chairman again interrupted.

'You have not told us, Mr Redfern, how you obtained these papers.'

'I said in the course of my work, sir.'

'That is not an answer, surely.'

'It is a fair answer.'

Llewellyn intervened. He made the expected point about the ethics of reporting, the duty to respect sources.

'In the case of papers such as these are alleged to be,' the Chairman said, 'it might be thought, Mr Llewellyn, that other ethics would apply.'

'If it will help,' I said, 'the papers reached me through the post. I do not know who sent them.'

Llewellyn, I noticed, looked angry as I said this. Perhaps it was only that I had spoken, as they put it, out of turn. The Chairman also looked angry but I could understand that.

'You have no evidence of their source?' he asked.

'None.'

'You did not keep the envelope? Or look at the post mark?'

'No.'

'That is surprising, surely. If you thought the papers important.'

'I didn't keep the envelope.'

'But you could have recovered it?'

'I'm afraid I didn't.'

'That is regrettable, surely.'

'Perhaps, from one point of view. But the source, then and now, was a secondary matter. I was and am more interested in the substance.'

The physical relations altered again. As I spoke, with more pressure, I felt the people in the room coming back into focus. Some feeling was coming through, from these crowded others who were watching. And we were now, finally, at the papers themselves.

I read them aloud. The room, while I was reading, went absolutely silent. It was mostly general material: reports on the situation at Pontyrhiw, on the power shortages, on the practical emergency arrangements. Then the passage that mattered came.

> It was agreed that recovery of the yard had become urgent. It was further agreed that any attempt at occupation was likely to be resisted. The Chief Constable's objections to the presence of military forces were, in this context, overruled. Mr Buxton proposed that the yard should be recovered, on the morning of 15 March. The first attempt should be made by the police, but with an infantry company in position to lend psychological support. If this attempt failed, further warning would be given and then the military would occupy the yard. It was agreed, after discussion, that this action might well involve some civilian casualties, if the illegal resistance, as seemed probable, continued. It was further agreed that, in the context of the emergency, this possibility must be accepted.

As I read these last words there was an even deeper silence and then, after a moment, a sound I can hardly define: a strange and seemingly collective sound: not at first of voices but of breath, the tension of breath. Then the spell was broken by a shout from the gallery: a single shout, 'Murderer'. There was again a silence, and people looked around, to see who had shouted. There were then more angry voices, and the Chairman started hammering, to recover control. But indeed control had not gone. The tension was still palpable, but there was more to hear and, under control, people were there to hear it. Llewellyn took me on to the next paper, Buxton's memorandum. All the early part was summary of the previous information, but then came the decisive words:

> I recommend immediate authorisation of this two-stage operation to recover the yard. The first stage, by the police only, has indeed to be executed, for general reasons, but is unlikely to succeed. The second stage, by the army, is not only, in reality, the necessary stage. It is in my opinion necessary also for broader reasons, to determine what has become an issue of legitimacy, in conditions of latent disorder on a wide scale, against which it must be seen that we are determined to act with all necessary force, accepting and indeed overriding the question of casualties. Harsh as this may be, or may appear to be, it is in practice no more than the final authority of government, and demonstration of this authority is now, plainly, a question of confidence.

So the climax was reached. I read the words out quietly, in the rational intonation that was Buxton's own substance and style. There was again a silence and a tension. Then an extraordinary thing happened. Bob James stood up.

'You murdered Gareth Powell,' he said, firmly.

We all stared at him. There was nowhere else to look. But the relations were so strange: who was he meaning by 'you'?

'Sit down,' the Chairman ordered.

He did not move. A policeman detached himself from the group by the door and walked towards him.

'Sit down and be silent or I shall suspend this Inquiry,' the Chairman ordered.

'You murdered Gareth,' Bob said.

He then slowly sat down. I went on watching him. His

234

resemblance to the photographs I had seen of Gareth was striking. And what he had said had emphasised this sense of strangeness, of some other kind of being. It was a voice from beyond the existing formal relations, but in what new relations I could not discern or decide. And the formal business was now being resumed: the lodging of the papers; Llewellyn's final formal questions; and then the Chairman's invitation to one of the official counsel, for cross-examination. I looked across at his neat, handsome face. I could feel his entire assurance. And all I knew, in myself, was another and deeper kind of questioning. I made the effort to attend and to answer.

'You claim to know nothing, Mr Redfern, of the source of these alleged documents?'

'They are not alleged documents. And of course I know their source. They are Cabinet papers.'

He smiled. He had been playing this patball for years.

'I meant their unauthorised source. Or if you find it difficult to understand my question, the name of the person or persons who unlawfully transmitted them to you?'

'I have already said, I know nothing about that.'

'Nothing? I see. So that nothing is known until we come to yourself?'

'I have presented, in the proper place, documents which came to me unrequested and anonymously.'

'I see. So that you have, in your own eyes, acted entirely properly?'

'I would listen, publicly, to any suggestion that I have not.'

'Would you, Mr Redfern? Then let me put this to you. When you received these documents you were, were you not, an employee of Insatel?'

'Yes.'

'A reporter, gathering news for the organisation which

235

employed you?'

'Those were not exactly my duties but in effect, yes.'

'Yet when you acquired these documents, which you would ask us to believe are important, you did not make them available to your employers?'

'No.'

'Why?'

'I decided that this Inquiry was the proper body to receive them. I thought they were too important to be confined to a private news organisation. There was a difference of opinion on this, and when it persisted I resigned.'

'I see. That is the reason, you say, that you resigned from your employment?'

'Yes.'

'Would it then surprise you to know that your employers state that the duties on which you were engaged had nothing whatever to do with this Inquiry?'

'No.'

'It would not surprise you?'

'Nothing much that they said would surprise me.'

There was a quick laugh in the room. I had provoked it, I suppose, but I didn't want it.

'You admit then, do you, that you were not working on matters connected with this Inquiry? And that the real reason for your abrupt resignation was your refusal of a perfectly normal request that you should carry out the work to which you were actually assigned?'

'They can say that, if they wish. The fact remains that I decided this matter was much more important.'

'I see. You made up your own mind. Can you tell us, perhaps, what you were actually working on?'

'No.'

'No? Why not?'

'It is a matter that has not yet been published. I have resigned, but I can still respect my former employer's confidence.'

'I see. But it is my information that what you were working on is very well known. It was the armed assault, at St Fagans, on Mr Edmund Buxton.'

It was like a hard blow to the stomach. I could feel my feet moving, involuntarily, and I struggled to control my face and my voice.

'No. That was earlier. That assignment was concluded.'

'Indeed? With what result?'

'With much the same result as the police inquiry. I reached the point they reached: the identification of the suspect as a Mr Marcus Tiller, who turned out to be an agent of an international body known as Political Research and Consultancy.'

'I see.'

He looked down at his papers. I saw an elderly man in the row behind him scribble a note and pass it forward.

'But that assignment, you say, was concluded?'

'Yes.'

I was watching the elderly man. He had neat grey hair and a very dark red complexion, with a small, bitter mouth.

'My employer explained,' I added, 'that in his judgement the attack on Mr Buxton was no longer of any particular interest, as public news.'

'I see. And you are still respecting his confidence, I take it?'

'So far as I can, consistent with answering your questions.'

Both the Chairman and Llewellyn were now evidently

restless. The more restless the better, so far as I was concerned. There was a brief pause. Counsel was looking at the note again, but then he folded it away.

'Your unexplained acquisition of these documents, then, is unconnected with your inquiry into the attack on Mr Buxton?'

'Yes,' I said. I wished, as I said it, that there could be an even shorter answer.

'Though the events themselves, in your opinion, might well be connected?'

'I have no evidence to show their connection.'

'And your motive in presenting these documents is similarly unconnected?'

'Motive is quite the wrong word.'

'What would your word be, Mr Redfern?'

I stood very straight and looked above his head. I spoke out clearly and plainly. 'I only wanted to help this Inquiry to arrive at the truth.'

He sat down on that. There had been a discrediting intention in his whole line of questioning, but it had gone wrong somewhere and the note, clearly, still puzzled him; probably no one had briefed him on Tiller.

I left the witness stand. I saw David Evans smiling down at me. His father, behind him, was again turned away. Many other people were smiling, and I could feel their approval.

But the real situation was very much harder than that. I had indeed presented a necessary truth. I had also, not once but repeatedly and consciously, lied. I knew all the arguments to justify this combination. I had no good arguments to refute them but I was still left tense and drained, and the last thing I wanted, now, was approval: a reduction of the process to some simple, positive, embracing act. And I was sick, also, as I saw, very clearly, the more general situation. We had established Buxton's complicity, and that was decisive. But no action ever runs a single course. The connections I had lied about, the radical connections that I had explicitly denied, were, in the end, of equal importance. Pontyrhiw and St Fagans were connected and must be connected. Each event and other events were connected, and must be connected, to a wider action, of which the Volunteers and others were themselves only elements. Meanwhile, from a different position, other connections were being run. Buxton's complicity, his euphemistic acceptance of the possibility of casualties, was at once being overlaid by the subsequent attack on him, which, in whatever else he had failed, my questioner had succeeded in reviving. In a matter of hours or days, doubtless planned to compete with this news of Pontyrhiw, the Volunteers story would break, and the scares would start, and the whole action would again be in movement, and there would be no end to it: no simple end, perhaps no end at all. All the rush and change of reality would bear in, necessarily, on what had been temporarily isolated as a particular action, a particular truth. To be there and to be telling it was a local moment, a significant moment, but the immense process continued, and there was no available identity outside it: only the process itself, which could never be properly told in any single dimension or any single place. There was only, now, the deep need to connect and the practical impossibility, for unregrettable reasons, of making the connections, even the known connections. Yet then, all the time, within this impossibility, were the inevitable commitments, the necessary commitments, the choosing of sides. Through the persistent uncertainty, within the

239

overwhelming process, I had now chosen and been chosen, in what would be, in effect, a quite final way.

John Davies and his friends came around me. When the Inquiry was adjourned we went out together, keeping the press at a distance. Still David managed to get near me and called over a shoulder: 'You left your dressing table tidy?'

'Sure. What else?'

'Sure. See you.'

We went down to the cars. We were due to go back to the offices, but I told John Davies I wanted to go to Pontyrhiw. He was surprised, but he arranged it. Bob James would give me a lift. There was a lot of handshaking before I left to walk to the car. I wanted him to hurry, as we walked to the car park, but he was easy and confident. It had been a victory, he said, and I couldn't disagree.

We drove back up the valley, on the busy road through the long terraced streets of the crowded townships. When we reached Pontyrhiw I asked him to go down Commercial Road and into Ferry Road. We stopped and looked at the gate of the depot. It was still shut. The fading chalk bullet marks were still on the walls along the street. A street in Pontyrhiw. A dirt road in Kenya. I must have gone silent, looking at them, because he said suddenly:

'You're trying to think back through it?'

'Yes, I suppose so.'

He waited a while. Then he offered to drive me to a meal. I said I wasn't hungry. It was true.

'How will you get back then?' he asked.

'I'm not sure. I'll get a train.'

'Well then I'll drive you to the station.'

I turned and shook his hand. It was a strong pressure.

'No thanks, Bob,' I said, 'I'll find my own way back.'

KIM HOWELLS

Kim Howells is a Labour Party politician and was a Member of Parliament for Pontypridd between 1989 and 2010. He was born in Merthyr Tydfil in 1946 and was educated at Mountain Ash Grammar school and Hornsey College of Art where he became involved in student politics.

Further to his work as an editor and researcher on *The South Wales Miner* he was employed as an official with the National Union of Mineworkers and was responsible for coordination of the union activity in Wales during the NUM national strike between 1984 and 1985. He served as minister in successive Labour governments between 1997 and 2009. He also chaired the Intelligence and Security Committee, a committee of parliamentarians that oversees the work of Britain's intelligence and security agencies.

STEVE BENBOW

Steve Benbow trained as a photojournalist at Newport College of Art and has travelled the world working for many of the leading magazines, including *Time*, *Newsweek*, *The Sunday Times* and *National Geographic*. He is founder of The photolibrarywales, which represents over 300 Welsh photographers and is the largest online catalogue of images of Wales available. He has recently diversified into documentary film making and is a director of Video Wales and Birdhouse Films.